vault

VOLUME I
OUT BEYOND THE DUST N' DARK

VAULT COMICS PRESENTS

WEST OF SUNDOWN

WRITTEN BY
TIM SEELEY & AARON CAMPBELL

DRAWN BY
JIM TERRY

COLORED BY
TRIONA FARRELL

LETTERED BY
CRANK!

CHAPTER
I

MANASSAS, VIRGINIA.
JULY 22, 1861.
SHNK
SHNK
SHNK

HNH. HNH. HNH.
COME ON.
SHNK

HNF. COME ON NOW. MAKE IT EASY WON'T YE...

...LAD?

DING
DING
DING

DING
DING
DING

DING
DING
DING

DING DING DING
JANEY MAC.

DING
DING
HEY! WHERE YA GOIN', YA *IRISH BASTARD?* BODIES'RE OVER HERE!
DING

DING
DING
DING
IN THE NAME OF THE FATHER...

SHNK
SHNK

PFUH! SPTT!
OH, MY.
SNF
SO IT SEEMS I'VE WOKEN IN THE MIDDLE OF DAVIS' LITTLE WAR.
I HAD HOPED TO SLEEP RIGHT THROUGH IT.
NOW, WHATEVER ARE YOU FIGHTING FOR?
I...
I DON'T KNOW.
THRMMMBL
WELL, THAT WON'T DO AT ALL, MISTER...?

O'SHAUGHNESSY.
DOOLEY O'SHAUGHNESSY.
SSKRAAKK
WELL, THEN, DOOLEY...

...WHAT SAY YOU WHISK MISS CONSTANCE DER ABEND AWAY FROM THIS AWFUL PLACE?
TO... TO WHERE?
"WHERE ELSE? WHY, TO NEW YORK CITY, OF COURSE."
A DECADE LATER.
ACADEMY OF MUSIC
WHAT HAS BECOME OF THIS PLACE?

INDIGENTS AND CATHOLICS EVERYWHERE.
HOMER, PLEASE, NOT NOW.
YOU WANT I SHOULD HELP?

HERE. BOOK YOURSELF PASSAGE BACK TO THE OLD COUNTRY WHERE YOU BELONG.
CLNK

WHY, YES, I DID HEAR! LEFT NOTHING TO HIS WIFE. POOR INGRID. BUT I HEARD THE HOUSE BOY GOT EVERYTHING HE WANTED, IF YOU TAKE MY MEANING.
HO! HO! MADAME ABEND, YOU'RE TOO MUCH.

I DO SO HOPE SHE SURVIVES THE FALL DOWN THE SOCIAL LADDER.
HE'S HERE, MISTRESS. HOMER G RUSSET.

THE ROBBER BARON CUNT WHO LET ALL A' THEM CHILDREN DIE IN HIS BUTTON FACTORY.
LOVELY, DOOLEY. LOVELY.

MISTER TWEED, WOULD YOU PLEASE EXCUSE ME?
CERTAINLY, MADAME. I DO HOPE, THOUGH, THAT YOU SHALL GRACE US WITH A BIT OF THE VALKYRIE THIS EVENING.
YOUR VOICE IS AS AN ANGEL'S.
"NE'ER FROM FOE HAD I FLED," MISTER TWEED.

♫ IN STRIFE LIKE THIS I TAKE NO DELIGHT;
♫ HOJOTOHO! HOJOTOHO! HOJOTOHO! HOJOTOHO! HEIAHA HA! HOJOHO! ♫
♫ TAKE WARNING FATHER, LOOK TO THYSELF;
STORM AND STRIFE MUST THOU WITHSTAND ♫
FRICKA COMES TO THEE HERE, DRAWN HITHER IN BY HER RAMS ♫
♫ HEI! HOW SHE SWINGS THE GOLDEN SCOURGE!
♫
THE WRETCHED BEASTS ARE GROANING WITH FEAR;
♫
WHEELS FURIOUSLY RATTLE;
♫
FIERCE SHE FARES TO THE FRAY
STAGE

SWEET THOUGH TO ME ARE THE FIGHTS OF MEN
♫ THEN TAKE NOW THY STAND FOR THE STORM; I LEAVE THEE WITH MIRTH TO THY FATE
♫ HOJOTOHO! HOJOTOHO! HEIAHA! HEIAHA! HOJOTOHO! HOJOTOHO! HEIAHA! HEIAHA!
LYE HANDLE WITH

HAHAHA.
OH, MY. HA! THEY CHEERED AND SWOONED WHILE I SPIT THE BLOOD OF ONE OF THEIR OWN BACK INTO THEIR FACES!
BRILLIANT!

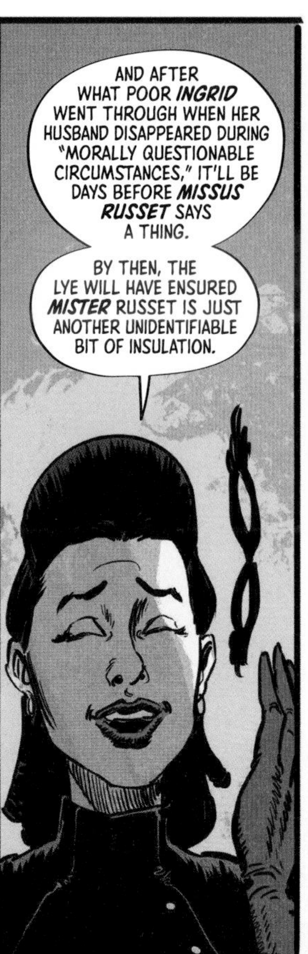
AND AFTER WHAT POOR INGRID WENT THROUGH WHEN HER HUSBAND DISAPPEARED DURING "MORALLY QUESTIONABLE CIRCUMSTANCES," IT'LL BE DAYS BEFORE MISSUS RUSSET SAYS A THING.
BY THEN, THE LYE WILL HAVE ENSURED MISTER RUSSET IS JUST ANOTHER UNIDENTIFIABLE BIT OF INSULATION.

THANK YOU, DOOLEY. TRULY. YOU HAVE MADE MY MEALS A GOOD DEAL MORE SATISFYING THESE PAST TEN YEARS.
AYE.
BUT... YOU DON'T SEEM PARTICULARLY JOYOUS ABOUT IT.

RUSSET'S A CUNT... WAS A CUNT, NO DOUBT. BUT SOMETIMES... IF I'M BEING HONEST, MA'AM...
I WONDER WHAT THE BLOODY HELL I'M DOIN'.
NOW, NOW.

YOU'VE BROKEN NO AMERICAN COMMANDMENTS THAT I CAN SEE. THIS IS A YOUNG COUNTRY, DOOLEY.
IT'S STILL DETERMINING WHO ARE ITS MONSTERS, AND WHO ARE ITS ANGELS.
THEN I'M GLAD WE LEFT BEFORE THE BALL GOT TOO "FRENCH." THERE'RE THINGS MY IRISH EYES WEREN'T MEANT TO SEE.
I'D EXPECT NOTHING LESS OF A GOOD CHRISTIAN BOY WHO BLUSHES WHEN I DO SO MUCH AS BEND OVER.

PERSONALLY, I FIND IT ALL LACKING IN IMAGINATION.
WHAT I COULD SHOW THEM, *EH,* DOOLEY?

DOOLEY?
MISS DER ABEND--
HALLO?! BITTE...

PLEASE. *SIE WERDEN NICHT AUF MICH HÖREN.*
DAS FEUER! DAS FEUER!

I'M SORRY. I DON'T SPEAK GERMAN, MA'AM.
THEY WON'T LISTEN TO HER, SHE SAYS. AS NEWLY ARRIVED AS SHE IS, I IMAGINE SHE'S QUITE RIGHT.
A ***FIRE.*** SHE SAYS THERE'S A FIRE--

EEEAGHK!

MISS DER ABEND?!
ACH DU MEINE GÜTE.
I FEEL IT... DEEP... DEEP WITHIN...

IT BURNS...

MY HOME BURNS.
MISS DER ABEND! *NO!*
MISS DER ABEND! PLEASE!
MY EARTH!
KAFF!
NO, MISS! YOU CAN'T. THERE'S NO SAVIN' IT!

NO! IT'S BEEN WITH ME TWO CENTURIES. MY NATIVE SOIL...

MY SOURCE. I...I CAN NO LONGER... FEEL IT.

DON'T YOU FRET, MISS. YOU SAVED ME FROM THAT MISERABLE WAR. YOU SHAN'T PERISH THIS NIGHT.

IT'S...IT'S DEAD, MIJITO. EVERYTHING I CREATED HERE, GONE. I WAS ACCEPTED. I WAS THE TOAST OF THE TOWN. EVEN EAKINS PAINTED ME.
WHY MUST THEY ALWAYS TAKE IT?
IT'S THE HUNTERS, MISS. THEY DON'T CARE THAT YOUR PREY BE FILTH. THEY HATE YOU JUST FOR BEING.
WE MUST GO, AN' WE MUST GO NOW.

I HAVE TO GO BACK, DON'T I? TO THE EARTH WHERE I WAS REBORN.
I had called New York home for the better part of a decade.
TO THE DOCKS THEN, MIJITO. YOU KNOW WHOM WE SEEK.
And with that, we went WEST.

The "midnight stevedores" at the port scarcely batted an eye. They'd moved human cargo before, and for a significant portion of Miss Der Abend's assets they ensured full passage aboard the clipper for the entirety of the ninety day journey to LOS ANGELES.
THOUGH I'LL SLUMBER, MY BODY WILL WASTE AWAY FROM HUNGER. IF I'M NOT FED AT SOME POINT...
...WHY, I MIGHT EVEN EAT YOU, DOOLEY.
I gave a small laugh. She was funny, Miss Der Abend.
I had been her constant companion these past years. She'd taught me to read and write and crave conversation about topics more interesting than God, fornicatin', and brew.
TAK TAK TAK TAK
But, as an outsider among both the crewmen and passengers, I had little choice but to conversate with myself in this journal...
...a document which doubles as a log to track what I believe may be the appearance of the hunters, still in dogged pursuit...
...or perhaps that's just distraction from reflectin' on this life I find myself livin'. This Bargain...

NOK NOK NOK
In New York, Miss Der Abend and I'd found a means for her to satisfy her hunger that appeased us both.
She fed upon those the Lord would bring charges upon. Whom deprived the poor of fair treatment. Whom made widows their prey and orphans their plunder.
There were none of those on this vessel.
Miss Der Abend was one of the strongest of her kind; lesser, she said, only to the great ROMANIAN COUNT. Yet still, she would need sustenance soon.
And so, I went to port in VALPARASIO.
I reckoned there would be a tyrant in this den of sin worthy of woe.

Or, at least, one who'd driven out the goodness of their spirit with debauchery and would have no need of their life blood.
HNNGH.

HNNGH. CONFEDERADO?
YOUR NEEDLE? IS IT FULL? PLEASE... MORPHINE.

JANEY MAC.
Instead, I found a victim trying to drown the pain of the body.
To forget his cowardness.

Maybe I'd have found another vein had I continued my hunt. But I'm a coward, too.

And I weren't the only hunter.

I'd traversed the world in my three decades, movin' e'er westward like my dutiful father.

I feared this might be my endpoint, failin' to serve my mistress, just as my father had failed to find the cairn of the fey folk that would grant his wishes.
NOK
NOK
NOK
NOK

It wasn't. The Clipper arrived in Los Angeles a full three months after our departure from New York.

But I knew our journey wasn't over, and there were still seven hundred miles of OLD SPANISH TRAIL left.

While purchasing the stagecoach, I made sure to loudly instruct the crewmen to be careful with the crate for it contained something of great value.
...FRAGILE, BEAUTIFUL, AND EXCEEDINGY RARE...

A beginner's mistake in a place so lawless as this. But I didn't lie.

Fragile. Beautiful. And exceedingly rare.

And though Miss Der Abend and I weren't widows or orphans...

...these men WERE the sort the Lord would bring charges upon.
HRRRCH!

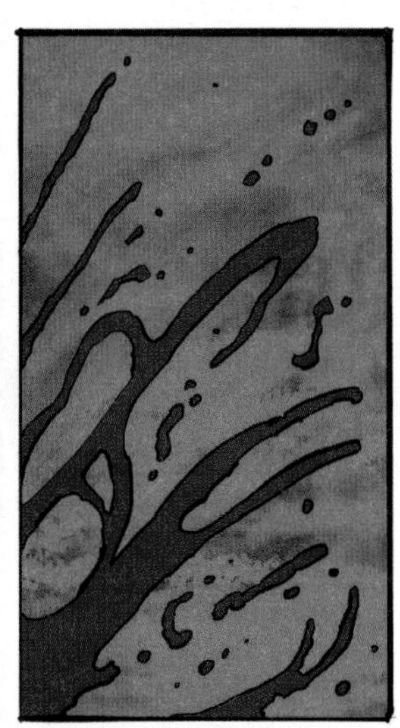

MISS DER ABEND.
DOOLEY. I CAN SMELL IT ON THE AIR. TASTE IT IN THE GROUND.

THANK YOU, *MIJITO.* IT'S CLOSE. THE SOIL OF MY HOMELAND.
SOON, I'LL RECOVER MY STRENGTH IN THE PLACE OF MY REBIRTH.
ALERT ME BEFORE WE ARRIVE. I SHOULD LIKE US BOTH TO LOOK OUR BEST UPON THIS OCCASION.
AYE, MISS.

I pulled the men off the road, so God and the crows might decide what to do with them.
TAK TAK

Which lead me to the conversation with myself I'd been avoiding. A conversation which must start at the beginning.
TAK TAK TAK TAK
TAK TAK TAK TAK

WELL, DOESN'T THIS BEAT ALL! I AIN'T SEEN THIS KIND A' RAIN UP HERE IN ALL MY YEARS.
GENERAL STORE
GENERAL STORE
I was born in IRELAND during THE FAMINE.

WHAT'LL YOU HAVE SHERIFF ABILENE?
A FIVE CENT GLASS AND SOME INSPIRATION, CUMBERLAND.
My mum had nothing but a crooked rifle and less to shoot at with it everyday.

ANOTHER CALIFORNIA WOMAN ASKIN' ME TO FIND HER HUSBAND--
THUM
THUM
THUM
THE HELL'S THAT NOW?
So, rather than see me starve, she brought me down to the river.

THUM
THUM
THUM
JUST BOUNCIN' BETTY DOIN' HER WORK 'FORE THE SHOOTIN' STARTS.
HM. YOU RECKON SHE'D MAKE A GOOD CHARACTER IN MY STORIES?
But as she placed me below the ripples, and I screamed in silent bubbles...

OR IS THAT NAME JUST A LIL' TOO CRASS FOR THE EAST COAST INTELLECTUALS WHAT WOULD BE MY AUDIENCE?
...she saw something. A VISION.

EXCUSE ME, SIR, WHAT'S THE NAME OF THIS ESTABLISHMENT?
HE THINKS YOU MEAN THIS PUBLIC HOUSE, DOOLEY. YOU MUST BE MORE SPECIFIC.
WHAT DO YOU CALL THIS RATHER... QUAINT TOWN, SHERIFF?
A RAVEN HAIRED ANGEL, who told her to let me live, because she'd watch over me.

SANGRE DE MORO, MA'AM. FOR THE MESA WHAT WAS HERE FIRST. IT'S QUITE A STORY, IF YOU SHOULD LIKE TO HEAR IT--
Years later, I came to this country with nothin' of my own, and found myself fightin' a war for five pennies a week.

"DE MORO." HOW FAMILIAR. MIJITO, GET ME A DRINK.
WINE INSTEAD OF THE USUAL. AND A BEER FOR YOURSELF.
I was looking for something. Anything. A sign.

Because, in trying to survive in this new country, I'd found few friends.

And, as my new countrymen had done, allowed myself to believe...

...it was my enemies who were immoral.

Now, my perspective has been realigned.

MISTER DIRCK.
THEY'VE ARRIVED, SIR. JUST BEHIND US, AS I SAID. MY MATH IS IMPECCABLE.
THANK YOU, MISTER GRIFFIN. THE PAIN ENDURED ON THIS LONG JOURNEY, IN THE BROKEN SHELL GIVEN ME BY MY FATHER, PROVES ITS WORTH...

...FOR IS IT NOT ALWAYS OF VALUE IN THE EYES OF GOD...
KREEEK

...TO ENSURE THAT THE UN-DEAD BE RETURNED TO THEIR GRAVE?
In this new country that has not yet decided who are its angels, I fear I can no longer tell...
...who are its MONSTERS.

CHAPTER
II

FORGOTTEN BY MOST.
"IT BEGINS AND ENDS IN THE CHAPEL OF SAN JUAN BATISTA, BELOW A DESERT MESA IN THE KINGDOM OF SANTA FE DE NUEVA MÉXICO.

"A SECRET WEDDING WAS HELD IN THE NIGHT--BETWEEN ISABEL NARANJO AND HER ONE TRUE LOVE, DOMINGO, A GENIZARO--BY A SYMPATHETIC FRANCISCAN PRIEST.

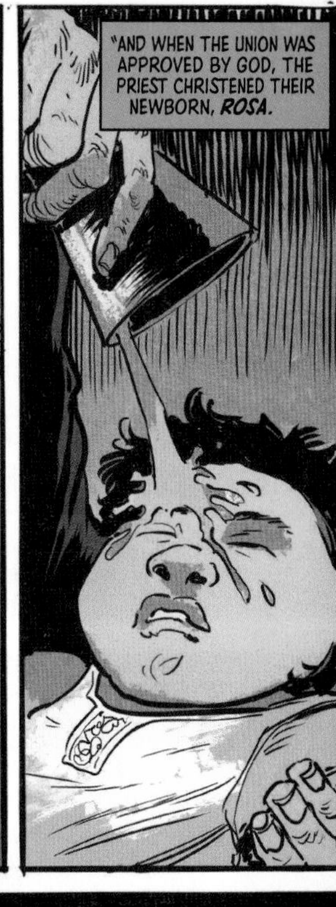
"AND WHEN THE UNION WAS APPROVED BY GOD, THE PRIEST CHRISTENED THEIR NEWBORN, ROSA.

"THEY WERE SO IN LOVE AND HOPELESSLY BLIND-- LOST IN DREAMS.
"THEY PROBABLY DIDN'T EVEN HEAR THE BARKING.

"HARDER, I THINK, TO IGNORE THE NEXT SOUND, LIKE A CLAP OF THUNDER."

"TO THINK, THEY WERE SO NAÏVE AS TO BELIEVE THERE'D BE NO CONSEQUENCES. IMAGINE, THE DAUGHTER OF THE GENERAL MARRYING A SLAVE. ALAS, YOUTH IS NOT KNOWN FOR ITS FORESIGHT.

"FRANCISCO NARANJO HAD BEEN AT THE EDGE OF THE KINGDOM FOR MONTHS, ONLY TO RETURN TO THIS--HIS HANDS NOW ACCUSTOMED TO LOADING HIS MATCHLOCK IN SECONDS.

"DOMINGO LUNGED FOR THE ARQUEBUS, WHILE HIS NEW WIFE HELD THEIR CHILD CLOSE--AWAY FROM THE SLAVERING JAWS OF THE GENERAL'S GIANT MASTIFF.

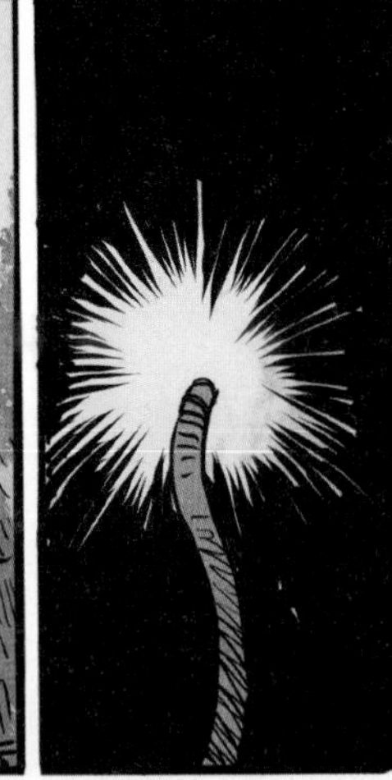

"ISABEL BREATHED PRAYERS--CERTAIN GOD WOULD SAVE THE MIRACULOUS BEING SHE HAD BROUGHT INTO THE WORLD."

"DOMINGO PULLED THE MATCHLOCK FROM THE GENERAL'S HANDS, AS THE WICK GREW SHORT."

ISABEL.

"THE BALL PASSED THROUGH THE HOUND'S BODY...

"...AND IMBUED WITH ITS BLOOD AND FLESH, FOUND ITS FINAL HOME IN ISABEL'S BREAST."
DIOS MIO.

"ROSA WAS BAPTIZED AGAIN, THIS TIME IN HER MOTHER'S BLOOD."

"DOMINGO WAS INSANE WITH GRIEF. HE RENOUNCED GOD IN *HIS* HOME. HE CURSED CHRIST'S NAME.
FWUMP
"THEN, RECALLING A TALE OF HIS YOUTH, HE TOOK THE DYING HOUND IN HIS HANDS. HE ASKED IT TO DO JUST AS IT HAD DONE TO ISABEL...
"...AND IMBUE HIM WITH ITS BLOOD AND FLESH.
"DOMINGO WAS NO MORE, AND THAT WHICH REMAINED WOULD BE CALLED *EL MORO*.
"BUT HE WOULD NOT WALK THE DARKNESS ALONE."

"LITTLE ROSA DID NOT CRY, FOR SHE WAS NOT HUNGRY.

"SHE HAD FED WELL ON HER GRANDFATHER'S BLOOD."

THAT WAS THE LAST SUNRISE I EVER SAW, DOOLEY O'SHAUGHNESSY.

THE GROUND NEAR THE MESA IS WHERE THE CHAPEL OF SAN JUAN BATISTA ONCE STOOD.
IT IS WHERE I WAS REBORN IN BLOOD. AND I MUST RETURN TO IT.
ROSA. I QUITE LIKE THAT NAME, MISS DER ABEND.

ROSA NARANJO IS LONG DEAD, REBORN AS THE MUCH MORE REFINED CONSTANCE DER ABEND.
BUT ROSA'S BIRTHPLACE HOLDS POWER. POWER I NEED TO REINVIGORATE MYSELF AND RETURN TO NEW YORK.

BUT FOR NOW, I MUST SLUMBER. FIND ME SUSTENANCE, DOOLEY. IT IS MORE IMPORTANT NOW THAN EVER.
YOU KNOW WHAT I LIKE.
MNNUH...

FAITH, **MISTER GRIFFIN.** FAITH AND TIMING.
THAT IS WHAT GUIDES OUR HUNT.

IT HAS BEEN A LONG JOURNEY, BUT THE SUN RISES, AND THE FIEND WILL BE AT HER WEAKEST.
WE WILL TAKE HER IN ***THE TEN CENT GLASS,*** WHERE SHE AND HER ADHERENT LIE.

WHEN HER DEMON HEART IS SENT BACK TO HELL, THE GOOD LORD WILL RECOGNIZE MY SERVITUDE AND OFFER LOVE AND FORGIVENESS TO A SON HE DID NOT FORM.

OH, MY, YES! WHAT ***TREASURES*** MUST LIE IN HER ANCIENT BODY, ***MISTER DIRCK.***
MISTER GRIFFIN... SOMETHING IS AMISS...
MY KNEES... I CANNOT... STAND WITHOUT...

SNAK
HNH! WHAT BELIEF DID I LACK, LORD?! WHAT PUNISHMENT IS THIS CURSED FORM?!
KRK
MISTER DIRCK? OH, MY! MY, MY!

THIS IS NO SANCTION, SIR. THIS IS SIMPLY THE GRADUAL DECLINE OF DECAYING THREAD.
BUT I AM PRACTICED NOW. THIS SHOULD DELAY US NO MORE THAN A DAY.
YES. *HNH.* YES, ANOTHER TRIAL, BUT I AM LEFT WITHOUT THE MEANS TO OVERCOME IT.

THAT IS HOW GOD DIFFERS FROM MY FATHER.
KRAK

YOU SEEMED IN SUCH AN IMPATIENT HURRY THESE PAST MONTHS. YET, YOU DO NOT SEEM DISAPPOINTED, MISTER GRIFFIN.
MY COMPLEXION COULD STAND ANOTHER DAY WITHOUT SUN. BESIDES, THOUGH I WAS LOOKING FORWARD TO STUDYING THE CRUEL HANDIWORK OF ***THE DEVIL***...

...YOUR ***VICTOR FRANKENSTEIN*** IS A NEAR SECOND.
RUNK
RUNK
RUNK

GENERAL STORE
THUM
THUM
THUM
10¢ GLASS

THUM
THUM
THUM
JUST BOUNCIN' BETTY DOING HER WORK BEFORE THE SHOOTING STARTS, MISTER O'SHAUGHNESSY.

I KNOW I ALWAYS ENJOY A YARN AFTER A GOOD REST. ALLOW ME TO TELL YOU HER TALE--
OR BETTER YET, HE CAN TAKE A "BOUNCE" FOR HIMSELF. STORIES DON'T PAY THE BANK, SHERIFF WOLFF.

COME ON NOW, CUMBERLAND! WHAT'S THE BOY NEED WITH A WHORE? DIDN'T YOU NOTE THE CALIBER OF THE WOMAN HE RODE IN WITH?
SHE LOOKED LIKE AN ETCHING FROM THE LUSTFUL TURK-- OR SO I'VE HEARD.

IT'S NOT... LIKE THAT WITH MISS DER ABEND. SHE--
I SAVED HIM.

CARRIED HIM AWAY FROM THAT AWFUL WAR AND OFF TO HIGH SOCIETY BALLS AND INDOOR PLUMBING.
COME NOW, DOOLEY. TIME IS WASTING.

LEAVING SO SOON?
WE'RE GOING TO THE MESA, SHERIFF, AND WE'LL BE ON OUR WAY TO LOS ANGELES BY MORNING.
THE MESA? WHATEVER FOR?

I SUFFER FROM SPELLS, SHERIFF. MISTER O'SHAUGHNESSY HAS ASSURED ME THERE IS AN HERB THAT GROWS NEAR THERE AT NIGHT KNOWN TO EASE THEM. A BIT OF "OLDE IRISH MEDICINE."
I THOUGHT IRISH MEDICINE WAS TWO SHOTS OF WHISKEY AND A PINT.

HEH. GOT TO WRITE THAT DOWN.
NOW LISTEN HERE. AS SHERIFF, IT'S MY DUTY TO WARN YOU THAT PEOPLE GO MISSING UP NEAR THAT MESA ALL THE TIME.

NEARLY EACH WEEK, I GET A TELEGRAM FROM SOME WIFE OR MOTHER ASKING ME TO GO OUT AND LOOK FOR A WANDERING TRAVELER. OF COURSE, WITH MY BUSY SCHEDULE...
"FEARLESS SONS OF ERIN."

THAT'S WHAT THEY CALLED THE IRISH WHO JOINED THE *UNION* ARMY. PROUD MEN. NEVER WOULDA LET THEMSELVES BE "CARRIED AWAY" FROM FIGHTIN' FOR ANOTHER MAN'S FREEDOM.

THERE WAS OTHERS, THOUGH. MERCENARIES WITH NO CONCERN BUT FOR THEIR EMPTY POCKETS.
I HEARD THEIR WAILS AND GAELIC CURSES AT GETTYSBURG. WATCHED GOOD MEN TAKE THEIR BULLETS.
GOOD MEN LIKE MY SON.

LET THEM GO OFF INTO THE WILDS, SHERIFF. THEY AIN'T WELCOME HERE NO MORE, ANYWAY.

WELL, NOW, IF YOU STILL THINK THE TRIP NECESSARY, I SUPPOSE I COULD OFFER MYSELF AS PROTECTION.
PERHAPS IN EXCHANGE FOR A STORY I MIGHT SEND TO ***HARPER'S?***
HA. OH, DEAR, SHERIFF. ***MY*** STORY WOULD HAVE TO BE LARGELY ***REDACTED***.
SHERIFF

BESIDES, I HAVE SPENT MANY YEARS IN ***NEW YORK CITY***, A DEN OF SIN AND VILLAINY IF ONE EVER WAS.

"I SHOULD THINK I CAN HANDLE WHATEVER NEW MEXICO MIGHT THROW AT ME."
IT'S QUITE A BEAUTIFUL PLACE, MISS DER ABEND. HARD TO IMAGINE SUCH A TERRIBLE THING AS YOUR STORY HAPPENIN' HERE.
HNNGH
MISS DER ABEND?
MY STRENGTH, DOOLEY. IT HAS BEEN TESTED BY THE JOURNEY. IF I DO NOT REST IN THE SOIL OF MY REBIRTH, I WILL HAVE TO FEED... MORE OFTEN...
...AND WITH NO CONCERN FOR WHOSE HOT BLOOD POURS DOWN MY THROAT!

THERE. THAT RIDGE. ON THE OTHER SIDE IS THE SITE OF MY BAPTISM.
IT'LL TAKE HOURS TO GET THE WAGON DOWN IT, MISS. YOU 'N' YOUR PRIDE... YOU DIDN'T TELL ME YOU FARED SO POORLY. IT'S IMPOSSIBLE NOW--

NO.
I'LL CARRY YOU.
IT CAN'T BE FAR NOW...

NOW.
HNGF
HNH

DOOLEY...

YOUR HEART. IT BEATS SO LOUDLY. SO... STRONG.
MISS...

...LOOK.
A RANCH.

POLLAS EN VINAGRE.
SOMEONE BUILT FUCKING STABLES OVER *MY* EARTH.

WHAT'S THAT STRANGE SOUND? LIKE CHAINS ON LEATHER.
JNGLKRAK
JNGLKRAK

SOMEONE IS HERE, DOOLEY.

"AND THEY ARE QUITE ENGAGED."
JNGLKRAK
JNGLKRAK

JNGLKRAK
JNGLKRAK
DO YOU HEAR IT WITHIN, BROTHERS AND SISTERS?! IT CALLS FROM WITHOUT!

IT SAYS, "THE BLOOD IS THE LIFE!" OVER AND *OVER* AGAIN!
BUT WHEN YOU HEAR IT, YOU ***MUST*** BEAT IT BACK! ***TAME*** IT WITH A WHIP!
THE BLOOD IS ***NOT*** LIFE! IT IS OF THE ***EARTH!***
EARTH IS FOR THE ***LOWLY THINGS!*** THE ***WORMS*** AND THE ***MAGGOTS*** AND THE ***SPIDERS!***

OUR SALVATION IS ABOVE! WE ARE OF THE HEAVENS! THE LIFE IS THE SKY!
KRAK
DAS LEBEN IS DER HIMMEL!
TUMP
MISS.
MISS?
BLASPHEMY! WHAT WOULD MY FATHER THINK OF SUCH DESECRATION TO THE PLACE WHERE HIS BELOVED WIFE BLED?!

MISS!
DOOLEY!

UUUOOOOT UUOOOOOT!

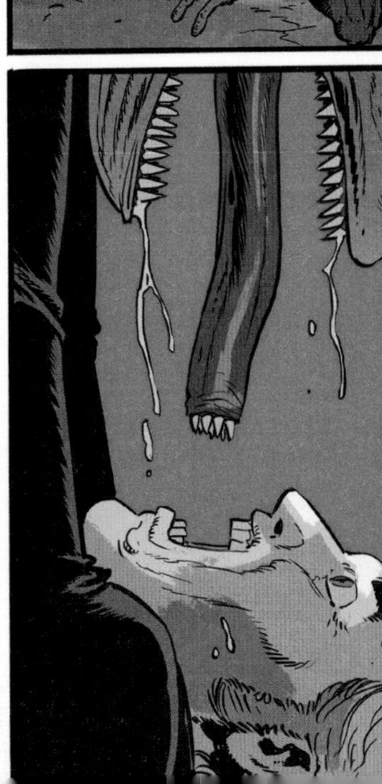
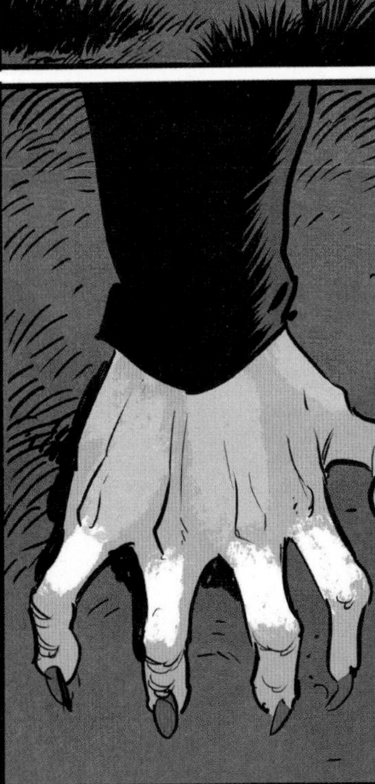

UUUOOOT UUOOOOT!
UUUOOORKK!
SHRORP
MY EARTH HAS FORTIFIED ME, BUT ONLY FOR A SHORT WHILE.
MISS. I'M... N-NUMB. THAT *OOTIN' THING'S* TONGUE...
SOME KIND OF PARALYTIC. MAKES FEEDING EASIER IF THE PREY CAN'T FIGHT BACK.

INGENIOUS REALLY.
UUUOOOT UUOOOOT!
UUUOOOT UUOOOOT!

THIS FLEETING STRENGTH MIGHT BE ENOUGH TO KILL THESE CREATURES AND PERHAPS EVEN THOSE FLAGELLATING FANATICS PROFANING MY EARTH.

BUT I FEAR IT WOULD DRAIN WHAT LITTLE I HAVE RECOVERED, AND I COULD NOT ASSURE YOUR SURVIVAL.

MISS?

I SUPPOSE I, AT THE VERY LEAST, OWE YOU YOUR LIFE, MISTER O'SHAUGHNESSY. I WILL CARRY YOU AS YOU HAVE ME.
BUT DO GRAB WHAT EARTH YOU CAN.

...SHE WAS EASILY THE MOST BEAUTIFUL WOMAN EVER TO STEP FOOT IN SANGRE DE MORO, BUT HER ODD OBSESSIONS DROVE HER TO THE MESA WHERE SHE--

WHUMP

OH, AH...MISS DER ABEND. BACK SO SOON?
MISTER O'SHAUGHNESSY AND I WILL BE STAYING FOR THE FORESEEABLE FUTURE.

THE HERBS WERE...NOT COOPERATIVE.
HNH!
THAT'LL BE SIX CENTS.

I ALREADY PAID. IT'S MINE.
THIS IS MINE, TOO.

IN FACT, THIS IS ALL MINE. I WOKE THE BANKER, WHO WAS MORE THAN HAPPY TO SETTLE YOUR DEBTS, MISTER MANOR.
A ROUND ON THE HOUSE TO YOU ALL!

AND DUE TO YOUR EARLIER TREATMENT OF US, YOU ARE FIRED, MISTER MANOR.

MISS DER ABEND...
SAVE YOUR THANKS, DOOLEY. HE INSULTED YOU.
AND I CAN'T VERY WELL KEEP ON OWING YOU FAVORS. NOW I'M AHEAD BY ONE, AND I LIKE IT MUCH BETTER THAT WAY.
MISS DER ABEND...

FUMP

SOMEONE WAS HERE, ***HERR JUNG***.

AND THEY DONE HIGHTAILED IT BACK TO TOWN AFTER DOING *THIS* TO ONE OF YOUR *PISCHACHAS*.
THIS LEVEL OF CURIOSITY IS FAR BEYOND THE PURVIEW OF *SHERIFF WOLFF*, WHO CAN RARELY BE BOTHERED TO WIPE HIS OWN ASSHOLE.
THE STRENGTH, THE SAVAGERY... MUSCLES PULLED APART RATHER THAN CUT.
THIS IS A NEW PLAYER, ONE WHO IS MOTIVATED TO COME TO OUR GROUNDS BY SOMETHING OTHER THAN THE LAW.
COME, *UNSIGHTLY ANNE*. WHEN OUR BELOVED MOON RISES AGAIN, LET US TAKE A TRIP TO *SANGRE DE MORO* AND VISIT OLD FRIENDS.
RRRRR...
WE MUST PROTECT OUR GODSEND AT ANY COST...
ROSA...?
...INCLUDING DRAWING FIRST BLOOD.

CHAPTER
III

SANGRE DE MORO. NEW MEXICO.
WHAT BLOODY HAPPENED?
10¢ GLASS
YOU DECIDED TO TAKE A NAP AFTER WE'D COME BACK FROM THE RANCH, DOOLEY.
UNFORTUNATELY, THERE WAS A HARD BAR BENEATH YOUR HEAD INSTEAD OF A PILLOW.
WE DID MANAGE TO RECOVER SOME SOIL, THOUGH. ENOUGH TO MAINTAIN SOME OF MY CONSIDERABLE STRENGTH, ANYWAY.
NOW, NO WRITING IN YOUR LITTLE BOOK. IT'S NEARLY DAWN, AND YOU'RE NO GOOD TO ME HALF-DEAD--
AAAOW!
MY, THAT IS ANGRY.
IT'S INFECTED. LORD KNOWS WHERE THE TONGUE OF THAT DAMNED "OOTIN'" FROG THING'D BEEN.
HM. WOULD YOU LIKE ME TO LICK IT?
WHAT?!
MY SALIVA IS QUITE ANTISEPTIC. A GIFT OF MY CONDITION.
COME HERE.

I--I THINK I JUST NEED SOME REST, MISS.
SUIT YOURSELF.

I OWN A SALOON NOW, SO WHEN THE MOON RISES, WE'LL DISCUSS ITS MANAGEMENT, AT LEAST UNTIL I OBTAIN MY ANCESTRAL GROUNDS--
THUM THUM THUM

OH, *HA.* WHAT A BUSY LITTLE BEE.
GOD. NOT THIS. ***ANYTHING*** BUT THIS.
HM. I SUPPOSE I SHOULD TALK TO OUR ***"SOILED DOVE"*** ABOUT OUR EXPECTATIONS AND THE NEW COSTS ASSOCIATED.
THUM THUM THUM

THUM THUM THUM
BETTY! ***BOUNCING BETTY!*** MISS...BOUNCING? OPEN UP RIGHT THIS INSTANT.

THIS CAN'T WAIT. YOU SEE, I'VE INHERITED THE TITLE OF "MADAM" WITH MY PURCHASE AND--
OH.
THUM THUM THUM

THUM THUM THUM
--AN' I CAST OUT ALL PAIN 'N' FEAR YONDER, BY THE GRACE A' FATHER'S LOVE!
WHY, HELLO THERE!
I'M--

MISS DER ABEND, YEAH, SURE, I HEARD! SHERIFF CAN'T GET YA OUT HIS MOUTH.
I'S JUST HELPIN' OL' BOOMER HERE WITH SOME PRAYER. GOT HIM A PECULIAR WOUND.
DON'T I KNOW YOU?
I...AH, NO--

COURSE YA DON'T, YA OL' FOOL. SHE ONLY BEEN HERE A FEW NIGHTS 'N' WHAT USE WOULD A LADY LIKE 'AT HAVE FER A POOR PROSPECTOR LIKE YOU? NOW GIMME 'AT NICKEL 'N' GIT ON!
THINKS T'WERE A DEVIL BIT HIM. I SAYS IT'S A BIG GODDAMN MOSQUITO. EITHER WAY, THOUGH, THE POWER 'A CHRIST'LL DRUM IT RIGHT CLEAN.

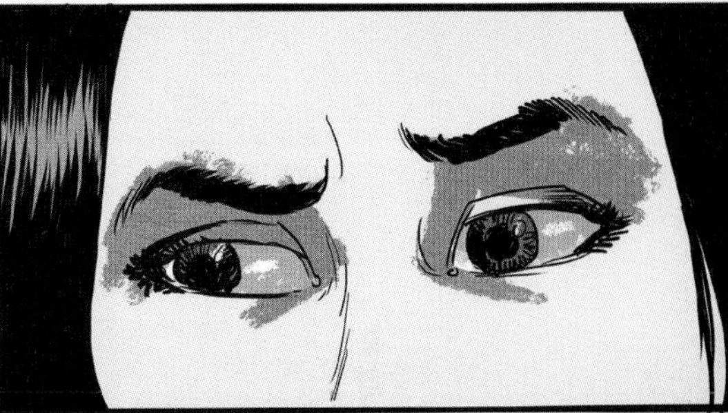

AHEM YES. THE THUMPING. YOU'RE A FAITH HEALER. I MISTOOK IT FOR--

OH, I FUCK 'EM, TOO. EIGHT DOLLARS A ROLL, TEN IF 'N' THEY WANT ANY A' THAT FRENCH STUFF. TWELVE IF I GOTTA DODGE BULLETS.
YOU WANT I SHOULD PAY YA MORE 'N' MY HALF SHARE FOR THE ROOM, MISS?

NO. NO, BETTY. YOU'RE VERY... CONVINCING.
LET'S KEEP THINGS AS THEY ARE.

"I COULD USE SOME PARTNERS IN THIS TOWN."
THAT BITCH. MAKING YOU REDUNDANT LIKE THAT.
COME ON, NOW, SHERIFF, YOU CAN'T GET ENOUGH OF HER.

BE THAT AS IT MAY, WHATEVER HAPPENS, I LIKE YOU. I'M GONNA PUT YA IN ONE A' MY STORIES, **CUMBERLAND.**
"BUFFALO SOLDIER, PARAGON OF THE NORTH!"
OH, JUST SO'S YA KNOW, YOU'LL BE WHITE.

WHAT ARE YOU DOING AWAKE, ***MISTER O'SHAUGHNESSY?*** THOUGHT YOU AND YOUR MISTRESS WEREN'T INCLINED TOWARDS THE DAY HOURS.
COULDN'T SLEEP. *HNF.* BUT YOUR SHERIFF WAS RIGHT ABOUT ONE THING...

...THIS ***IS*** A BIT OF "OLDE IRISH MEDICINE."
HNGH

WELL, IT'S YOURS NOW. THE WHISKEY AND THE GLASS.
I'M OFF TO THE HOTEL, UNTIL I FIND WORK.
LOOK, ***MISTER MANOR.*** I'M SORRY. WHAT YOU SAID, ABOUT YOUR SON... WELL, CONSTANCE, SHE CAN BE RASH.
I DON'T EVEN KNOW HOW A BAR CAN MAKE MONEY IN A PLACE WITH MORE BUILDINGS THAN PEOPLE. WHAT I'M SAYIN' IS... IT WASN'T MY CHOICE TO SEND YOU OFF.

YEAH, PEOPLE SAY THAT. BUT IN MY EXPERIENCE, PEOPLE WHO DON'T LIKE TO MAKE CHOICES JUST FIND SOMEONE WHO'LL TELL THEM TO DO THE THINGS THEY WANTED TO DO ANYWAY.
HAPPY TRAILS, MISTER O'SHAUGHNESSY. BEST ORDER SOME MORE TAOS LIGHTNING. YOU'RE RUNNIN' LOW.
ME, I MIGHT TRY WORKING THE LAND.
FIGURE IT CAN'T BE MORE DUPLICITOUS THAN PEOPLE.
HA.
WHO'S--?
...
YOU.
FROM NEW YORK.
INDEED. THOUGH GRIFFIN IS A MAN OF THE WORLD.
HA HAHAHA HAHAHA HA!
JESUS, MARY--

--'N' JOSEPH.
HAHA-- AHK!
DONK

HUNTERS. OH, BOLLOCKS. MISS DER ABEND.
HNNH.

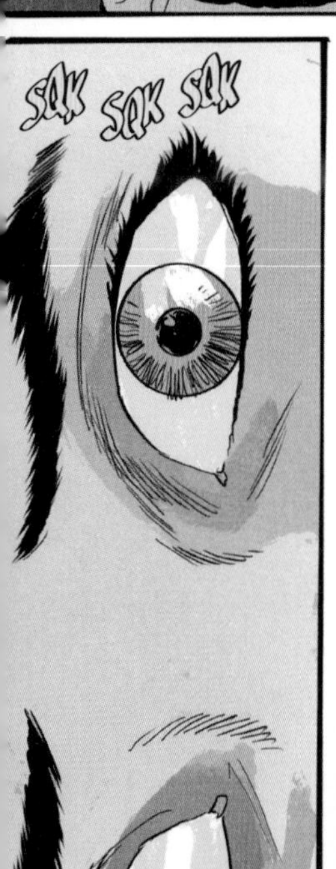
SQK SQK SQK

HMH?
SQK SQK SQK

DOOLEY?

HOW I MISS MY QUIET NEW YORK CITY.
SQK SQK SQK

SQK
SQK
SQK

SQK
SQK
SQK

LORD, LET ME TAKE THE FIEND'S HEART!
AHNGH!
SLSH
YOU POSSESS THE UNHOLY SPEED OF SIN! BUT IT MATTERS NOT.
WHETHER YOU BURN IN THE SUN OR BY FLAME LIKE THE LOAM THAT SUSTAINED YOU, YOU SHALL BURN JUST THE SAME!

YOU'RE THE HUNTER WHO DESTROYED MY HOME. MY *LIFE.*
YOU'LL CHOKE ON ME, YOU SHRIVELED OLD LEPER.
MISS!

I'VE GOT THE BASTARD.
WHAM

GODDAMNIT! WORDS COME OUT MY MOUTH BUT NEVER OUT MY FUCKING PEN!!

BLAM
HNH?!

GUN FIGHTS IN MY TOWN? BY THE LORD HARRY...
...NOT WITHOUT PROPER DOCUMENTATION.

AH. BOLLOCKS.
HE MISSED. THE LORD SANCTIONS ME NO MORE.
OH, HELL, DOOLEY...

MY BLESSING IS YOUR DOOM, ADHERENT!

CLEARLY, WE'VE NOT SPENT ENOUGH TIME AT THE RANGE, DOOLEY.
ALAS, I SHALL MAKE DO!
VAIN THING!
WHILE YOU FEIGN CONCERN FOR YOUR BONDMAN--
--YOU LOSE YOUR ONLY ADVANTAGE.
KRAK

MADRE DE DIOS. THAT POOR WOMAN...

SHE'S NOT ONE OF OURS. BEST YOU GET OUT THE STREET, UNDERTAKER.
YOU'LL HAVE TIME TO OGLE HER UNDERGARMENTS WHEN SHE'S IN A BOX.

Y-YOU WON'T HAVE ME. MY FATHER MADE ME STRONG. I ALWAYS SURVIVE.
GUH. SO IT APPEARS, INDECENT BEAST. STILL YOU SEEK SHADOWS AS THE LIGHT OF GOD TAKES YOUR HELL-BORN STRENGTH.
BUT THAT SAME LIGHT FILLS ME WITH THE HOPE OF WHICH I WAS ONCE ROBBED.

AND I WILL SEE THAT GIFT REPAID...
SNAK

...WITH YOUR ANNIHILATION.

NO NEED TO MAKE IT QUICK, MISTER DIRCK! DISCOVERY NEED NOT EXCLUDE PAIN!

'EY, YOU SLEEVEEN!
WOK

AWAAAO.

GOD.

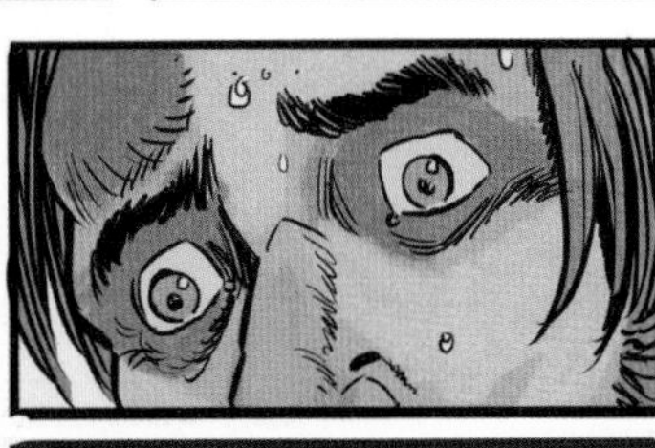

YOU'RE JUST A BOY--

POK
POK
POK
POK
POK

NO MERCY FOR THE ACCOMPLICES OF BLASPHEMY.
BRAAAAAP

JANEY MAC.

MISTER "DIRCK", IS IT?
HRNNK!

YOU THOUGHT TO DRIVE ME FROM MY WORLD OF COMFORT AND CULTURE.
HUNT ME WHILE I WAS OUT OF MY ELEMENT IN THIS HUSK OF A TOWN.

BUT YOU SHOULD KNOW, STITCHED-MAN, I AM HOME...

KRAK

...WHEREVER THERE IS DARKNESS.
MY NAME. DIRCK. IT COMES FROM AN ARTIST I SAW IN A GALLERY IN UTRECHT.
HE HAD DONE A PAINTING OF PROMETHEUS BEING STRAPPED TO A ROCK FOR GIVING FIRE TO HUMANITY.

NNNH. IT WAS BEAUTIFUL. EXPERTLY COMPOSED. LIGHT DANCING ACROSS FLESH. A PRIME EXAMPLE OF MAN'S CAPABILITY FOR CREATION.

KRATCH

GUH. A--A REMINDER OF MY OWN PUNISHMENT AS MODERN PROMETHEUS.

SHUK
AND OF THE FIRE THAT STILL RUNS THROUGH MY VEINS.

HUK!

NOT JUST FIRE. AS PART OF MY CREATION, MY FATHER FOUND IT NECESSARY TO ADD A MORE CONDUCTIVE MATERIAL TO MY BLOOD. A METAL.
SILVER.
NOW, CREATURE, LET US SEND YOUR SOUL TO THE DEVIL...
10¢ GLASS

...AND YOUR BODY UNDER MISTER GRIFFIN'S SAW.

THRMMMB

Sometimes, in times like these, I think of my mum and dad.

Goin' through their own lives, my father lost in a world of his own making...

...my mother trapped in the one he left her when he disappeared.

I wonder, were they alive right now, what they would think of this life I've come to inhabit.

PFH. A BOY. HA. I'LL BE THE MAN OF THE HOUR SOON ENOUGH!

Would my father still believe all his problems could be whisked away by fey folk, if he knew what kind of beings really lived in the secret places?
Would my mother still believe the raven-haired angel would save my soul?

Or would she think the world would have been better off if God had taken me down the river?

BLAM
CURSE MY GODDAMN PIG-FUCKING **RED EYES!**

THWAK
GHK!
GOT YOU THAT TIME, YE TOOL! MISS DER ABEND--!
GENERAL STORE
HNGH!

RIDE, DOOLEY. TO MY SOIL. IF I'M NOT IN TOUCH WITH MY GROUND, I'LL DIE.
BUT THOSE THINGS, MISS! *THE OOOTERS!*

GO AROUND THE BACK OF THE MESA, DOOLEY. AVOID THE RANCH. I'VE NO CHOICE NOW.

SANGRE DE MORO WILL HAVE ME ONE WAY OR ANOTHER.

HOO DOGGIES. TO HELL WITH HARPER'S.

JOURNAL
D. O'SHAUGHNESSY

I'LL BE THE KING OF THE GODDAMN PENNY DREADFULS!

CAN I GET YA ANYTHING ELSE, MISTER MANOR?
NO, SUSIE, THAT'LL BE QUITE ENOUGH.
WHAT A WILD DAY! SHOOTIN'S, AN' TUMBLIN' ABOUT ON THE STREET!
LIKE LIVIN' IN SANTA FE, AINNIT?
I DON'T KNOW, AND I CAN'T SAY I RIGHT CARE. THIS PLACE HASN'T GOT ANYTHING IN IT FOR ME ANYMORE.
OH MY! CUMBERLAND! COME LOOK!
LOOKS LIKE THE EXCITEMENT AIN'T DONE WITH US!
HERZOG.

COME ON NOW, BETTY. MOVE ASIDE, *SENÓR* VALDEZ.
SHERIFF COMIN' THROUGH.

AHEM
HOWDY, **REVEREND.**

I'M LOOKING FOR SOMEONE. A STRANGER TO TOWN. RECENTLY ARRIVED I'M TO ASSUME. UNUSUAL. UNIQUE.
GIVE THIS PERSON UP TO ME, AND WE WILL LEAVE AS QUIETLY AS WE CAME.

AH, WELL, I SEE YOU ADDED A SUBSTANTIAL NUMBER TO YOUR NEW CONGREGATION SINCE LAST WE SAW YOU.
GUESS I KNOW WHAT TO TELL ALL THEM WIVES 'N' MOTHERS BACK IN CALIFORNIA NOW.

IN ANY CASE, WE ALL KNOW A' WHO YOU SPEAK, AN' BEIN' THAT YOU GOT SOME HISTORY WITH THIS TOWN, I'LL TELL YOU THAT SHE AIN'T HERE RIGHT NOW, BUT IF YOU JUST PULL UP A--
NO!

SEEMS I RECALL YOU LEAVIN' US HIGH 'N' DRYER 'N' A PEPPERMINT FART, **REVEREND JUNG.**
=AHEM=
THIS TOWN AIN'T GOT MUCH, BUT WHATEVER WE DO GOT, WE DON'T OWE IT TO YOU.
YOU'NS 'N' YOUR'N **"POOLIES"** CAN GO STICK CHITS UP YOUR'NS ASSES.

HM. I'LL TAKE IT THIS LITTLE GNAT OF A WHORE DOESN'T SPEAK FOR THE REST OF YOU?
SHE SPEAKS FOR ME.

YOU CAME TO THIS TOWN OFFERING US SALVATION, REVEREND. SAID YOU WANTED TO EASE THE PAIN IN OUR HEARTS.

INSTEAD, SANGRE DE MORO WAS NOTHIN' MORE TO YOU THAN A LOW RUNG ON A LADDER.

AND YOU TOOK OUR SALVATION WHEN YOU SPLIT OUR FAMILIES IN TWO AND WALKED OFF INTO THE DESERT TO GO YELL AT THE MOON.

INDEED! WE STAND BY OUR OWN, YOU MOTHER-STEALING HUN PERVERT!
PINCHE PENDEJO!
NOW, WAIT JUST A MINUTE...

MISTER MANOR, WHAT I OFFERED YOUR WIFE AND OTHERS WAS SOMETHING THIS SPECK OF DIRT NEVER COULD. I SHOWED THEM A FUTURE.
THE WORLD IS ADVANCING FASTER THAN ITS INHABITANTS. CATASTROPHE WILL FOLLOW.

I HAVE GIVEN YOU AMPLE OPPRTUNITY TO JOIN US. I HAVE BEEN PATIENT.
BUT INTERLOPERS AND SABOTEURS COME FOR MY PEOPLE IN OUR SACRED HOME. THEY KILL OUR *PISCHACHA* GUARDIANS.

IF YOU WILL NOT BE OUR CONGREGANTS, YOU WILL BE OUR *FUEL.*

BROTHERS AND SISTERS...

...DAS LEBEN IS DER HIMMEL!

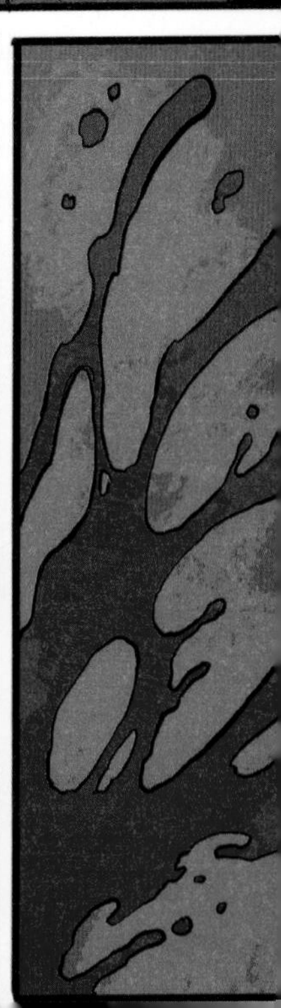

CHAPTER
IV

OH, BLOODY HELL.
WE'RE STUCK IN A CARCASS.

MISS DER ABEND? HELLO, MA'AM? I HATE TO BOTHER YE, SINCE YOU JUST ENDURED AN ATTACK BY VICIOUS HUNTERS AND ALL, BUT WE'VE GOT A BIT OF A PREDICAMENT.

hnnf
DOOLEY. DID WE NOT FLEE ***SANGRE DE MORO*** IN THE LATE AFTERNOON?
HMM. YEAH.
IT SHOULD BE AFTER DARK. AND WE SHOULD BE UPON THE STABLES BY NOW.
WE SHOULD BE UPON ***MY SOIL.***

I WENT AROUND THE MESA TO AVOID THEM OOTIN' CRITTERS.
hnnf
BUT WE WERE HERE JUST LAST NIGHT. I COULD'NA GOT US LOST.
MY SOIL. I SENSE THAT IT'S NOWHERE NEAR. BUT MY WOUNDS ARE HEALED.
AND I FEEL TREMENDOUS. LIKE I'M BATHING IN A WARM POOL OF DARKNESS.
RNNNCH
HM. I THINK I SHOULD LIKE TO SEE THAT.

TAME YOUR ADOLESCENT SYMPATHIES, **MISTER GRIFFIN.**
THE WRETCH IS AT THE END OF HER UNNATURAL LIFE. NOW, WHILE YOU FIND OUT WHAT SHE IS MADE OF...

I SHALL SHOW HER BONDSMAN WHAT I KNOW OF PAIN.

GOD SAVE ME, HE LOOKS SERIOUS, MISS.
DOOLEY, NEVER MIND THEM. THEY AREN'T IMPORTANT ANYMORE.
THE SKY. MY SOIL. I KNOW WHY WE'RE LOST!

THOSE WHO IGNORE ME OFTEN FIND IT TO BE THEIR LAST MISTAKE...
REISMULLER.
TH-THAT NAME. I KNOW THAT NAME.
KARL. *KARL REISMULLER.*

DIRCK? WHO ARE YOU TALKING TO?
THAT... THAT NAME, GRIFFIN. IT WAS ON A FRESH GRAVE IN INGOLSTADT.

I HAVE LONG BELIEVED... IT IS THE NAME OF THIS FLESH I OCCUPY.
BLOODY HELL, MAN. ARE YOU IN ONE OF YOUR FEVERS? SNAP OUT OF IT OR--!
HA. HAHA. PALE AS A GHOST. HA.

NO.
GHOSTLY GRIFFIN.

I LEFT YOU ALL BEHIND IN LONDON.
NO!

HNNF
DOOLEY! RUN! FAR AND FAST AND DON'T LOOK BACK!
BUT, THE NAG--

NEIII
SHRRRP

NEIIIII
LISTEN! THE REASON I CAN'T FEEL MY EARTH, DOOLEY...
OH GOD!
SHRRRP
SHRRRP
...IS BECAUSE WE ARE NO LONGER OF THE EARTH!

SANGRE DE MORO.

HNUUH
HNUUH
HNUUH
HNUUH

S'QUIET. NOT EVEN THE THUM THUM THUM OF BOUNCIN' BETTY'S EVENIN' SHIFT UPSTAIRS.
REVEREND HERZOG AND HIS CONFOUNDED CONGREGATION GOT 'EM ALL.

ALL EXCEPT ABILENE WOLFF. NO, SIR. I RAN THE DEATH GAUNTLET LIKE BUFFALO BILL IN KING OF THE BORDERMEN AND COME OUT ALIVE.
AN' NOW, AIN'T NO REASON NOT TO RUN FAR AS I CAN GET, 'CUZ I GOT THE KEY TO ALL MY FUTURE SUCCESSES. I GOT THE BOOK.

I GOT THE...
SON OF A BITCH.
SON OF A BITCH!!

I BET YOU LIKE TYIN' ME UP, DON'T YA? WELL, ENJOY IT.

'CUZ HERZOG IS FUCKIN' YOU POOLIES HARDER 'N' EVEN BOUNCIN' BETTY EVER COULD.
QUIET, WHORE.

HOW? AFTER ALL WE'VE BEEN THROUGH, JOANN, HOW COULD YOU DO THIS TO YOURSELF?
TO ME?!

CUMBERLAND, I... JUST WANTED A FUTURE... FOR US BOTH.
IS SOMETHING TROUBLING YOU, MY DEAR?
REVEREND, I WANT TO GIVE MY HUSBAND TO THE ETERNAL SKY. LET HIM HEAR THE WORD OF THE GODSEND.

NO, FRAU MANOR. I AM AFRAID IT IS TOO LATE. HE AND THE OTHERS WERE OFFERED A CHANCE TO HEAR THE VOICE--FROM WITHOUT AND WITHIN.
THEY SPIT ON US. THEY RAN US OFF LIKE DOGS IN THE NIGHT. AND THEY CLUNG TO THEIR SILENT GOD.

YOUR THOUGHTS ARE CLOUDED BY THE POWER OF THE VOICE, FRAU. BEAT IT BACK. TAME IT. AND AWAIT THE SALVATION EARNED BY YOUR REJECTION OF TEMPTATION.
Y-YES, REVEREND.

I CAN TASTE YOUR SWEAT ON MY TONGUE, **HERR JUNG.** YOU'RE WORRIED.
MY CONGREGATION IS TESTED. TO TAKE IN THEIR NEIGHBORS, EVEN BY FORCE, WAS NOT SO MUCH TO ASK...

...BUT TO ASK THEM TO BLEED THEIR LOVED ONES LIKE PIGS MAY TAKE A PERSUASIVENESS ONLY THE **GODSEND** HAS.
WELL, SEE, THAT'S WHERE I MIGHT BE ABLE TO HELP.

BACK IN TOWN, I WAS CHASING DOWN **SHERIFF WOLFF.** HE WAS A'SCREAMIN' AND A-HOWLIN' LIKE A BANSHEE, TOSSIN' EVERYTHING HE COULD BACK AT ME. SAND DONE FUCKED UP MY **LENSES** SOMETHIN' GOOD.

SO I WAS STUMBLIN' BLIND WHEN SOMETHING HIT ME FULL ON THE HEAD. A BOOK. THE SHERIFF RUN FASTER 'N' A GREASED PIG, BUT I PICKED UP THAT BOOK HE CHUCKED AT ME.

EVEN AFTER MY ACCIDENT, I STILL LIKE ME A GOOD YARN. AND THE DIARY OF MR. O'SHAUGHNESSY?
IT'S REAL **GODDAMN** INTERESTING.
RRRRRR.

YOU WEAR THIS PALLID FLESH, STOLEN FROM A DEAD MERCHANT FAT ENOUGH TO WRAP AROUND YOUR GIANT FRAME.

BUT THE FRAME IS EMPTY--SAVE FOR CHEMICALS.
YOU ARE A SOULLESS PLAYTHING FOR THE BOY. THE SICK BOY WHO RE-BUILDS YOU IN AN IMAGE THAT SCOFFS AT GOD.

SICK BOY. *HA. HAHA.*
YOU LAUGH LIKE THE OTHERS?!

HOW DARE YOU LAUGH AT ME AFTER ALL I'VE DONE FOR YOU?!
SLSH

I LAUGH BECAUSE I FINALLY SEE WHAT I HAVE IGNORED... THE DELIGHT IN YOUR EYES WHEN YOU SPLIT MY BONES AND STITCH MY FLESH! I WILL NO LONGER BE A PROFANE TESTAMENT TO YOUR PERVERSIONS, MR. GRIFFIN!!
GHK!

GHK!
SHRAKOOM

I COULD DO IT SO EASILY, DOOLEY. I COULD FILL THE ALBINO'S LUNGS WITH RAIN. I COULD SEND LIGHTNING THROUGH THE PIECEWORK MAN. WE COULD FIND OUT HOW CONDUCTIVE THE SILVER IN HIS BLOOD IS THEN.
BUT, DOOLEY, I'M SO STRONG HERE!
NO, MISS! WE JUST NEEDED THE THUNDER TO DROWN THE VOICES!
IF WHAT YOU SAY IS TRUE, WE'LL NEED ALL THE LIVIN' BLOODY SOULS WE CAN GET!

HNH.
MY EARS RING LIKE A SUNDAY MORNING.
GOOD. SHOULD KEEP THE WHISPERS OUT FOR A BIT.

I'M GUESSIN' YOU UNDERSTAND WE SAVED YOUR LIVES, EVEN AFTER YOU TRIED TAKIN' OURS.
WELCOME TO THE OTHER SIDE OF THE VEIL, YEAH?

WHAT NONSENSE DO YOU SPEAK?
NO NONSENSE. FOR THOUSANDS OF YEARS, NATIVES BELIEVED THE MESA WAS A PATH TO THE LAND OF THE MOON, ACCESSIBLE BY THE DREAMS OF THE SHAMAN, OR ON HOLY NIGHTS WHEN THE BORDERS THINNED.
AND WHETHER YOU BELIEVE IT MATTERS NOT, AS I HAVE PROOF OF THE INFLUENCE OF FORCES FROM BEYOND ON... HUMAN MATTERS.
YOU. YOU ARE A PRODUCT OF THIS UNHOLY PLACE. WHAT FAUSTIAN BARGAIN HAVE YOU MADE, SHE-DEVIL, IN BRINGING US TO ***HELL?!***
YOU FOLLOWED ME, YOU SINGLE-MINDED FOOL! YOU WALKED THROUGH THE VEIL OF YOUR OWN ACCORD!

SHE'S RIGHT! SO STOP BLAMIN' OTHERS, ESPECIALLY WHEN THE ONLY WAY OUT IS BY FOLLOWIN' MISS DER ABEND!
BLOOD. I SMELL IT ON THE AIR. THAT MEANS PEOPLE. THAT MEANS THE RANCH.

AND WHY WOULD WE TRUST THE BONDSMAN OF A BLOOD-DRINKING WRAITH?
WELL, IF YOU'LL REMEMBER, "GRIFFIN," I HAD YOU DEAD TO RIGHTS BACK IN TOWN AND I LET YOU LIVE. AND, SECOND...

...WHILE THOSE VOICES WERE MAKIN' YOU MAD ENOUGH TO KILL EACH OTHER, THE ONE I HEARD BELONGED TO MY FATHER.
IT WAS SOMETHIN' HE ALWAYS USED TO SAY WHEN HE PUT ME DOWN TO BED.
"IF YOU FIND YOURSELF LOST IN TH' LAND OF THE FEY, *MO MHAC*..."

...KEEP YOUR EYES WIDE AND WALK A STRAIGHT LINE. IF YOU DON'T EVER STRAY FROM THE PATH, NO MATTER WHAT YOU'VE WALKED THROUGH IN YOUR DAYS...

"...YOU'LL COME OUT IN A BETTER PLACE."

NOW, COME ON. WHETHER IT'S THE LAND OF THE MOON, HELL, OR THE FAERIE KINGDOM, YOU LOT GOT HERE CHASIN' YOUR DEMONS...
...AND IF YOU STAY HERE, YOUR DEMONS WILL CHASE YOU.

HNNNH.
COME...
...FALL...
NNN--
DAMN **MISERABLE FLESH!** DAMN MY BONES!
FALL!
FALL!
MIGHT BE EASIER TO STAY ON THE PATH IF YOU LEAVE THAT BIG GUN BEHIND. WON'T DO ANY GOOD AGAINST THE THINGS IN THE SHADOWS, ANYWAYS.
YE CAN'T SHOOT WHAT DON'T HAVE A BODY.

I WILL STAY THE PATH ***AND*** KEEP MY ARMAMENT. THE PUCKLE NEED ONLY WORK ON YOU AND THE DEMON-BITCH, BONDSMAN.
I'D TAKE YOUR MISTRUST PERSONALLY, BUT THAT SIDESHOW BACK THERE TELLS ME YOU DON'T EVEN TRUST YOUR LITTLE RIDIN' COMPANION.

MR. GRIFFIN HAS DONE ME A GREAT DEAL OF PAIN, ***MR. O'SHAUGHNESSY.***
BUT IT WAS AT MY REQUEST.

FOR DECADES, I HUNTED THE DEVIL'S SPAWN IN FORESTS AND CAVERNS, LEFT THE BISECTED FORMS OF *DRAUGRS* OUTSIDE SLEEPING HAMLETS.
BUT THE DEMONS BEGAN MOVING TO THE NEW WORLD. TO BLOSSOMING CITIES. TO ***AMERICA.***

MY CREATOR FORMED ME AS A TESTAMENT TO HIS OWN EGO. I TOWERED OVER BORN-MEN. MY HEIGHT MADE ME AN OUTSIDER. IT IMPEDED MY GOD-GIVEN MISSION.

I FOUND MR. GRIFFIN IN A MANHATTAN ALLEY, PERFORMING ILLICIT SURGERIES FOR BRIGANDS AND PIRATES. MERELY A CHILD, BUT POSSESSING A FIRE FOR DISCOVERY I HAD ONCE SEEN IN MY CREATOR.

I ASKED HIM TO REMOVE NEARLY A YARD OF BONE AND MUSCLE FROM MY BODY, AND STITCH WHAT REMAINED BACK TOGETHER.
JANEY MAC.

AMERICA DEMANDS GREAT SUFFERING FROM OUTSIDERS BEFORE IT WILL LET THEM IN, MR. O'SHAUGHNESSY.
HUMAN SACRIFICE.

YOU'RE BEAUTIFUL, YOU KNOW?
YES, I DO KNOW. AND HAVING MY FLESH OGLED BY A CRETIN IS NOT THE COMPLIMENT YOU THINK IT IS.

NO, NO, YOU MISUNDERSTAND, MISS DER ABEND. I SEE YOU FOR WHAT YOU TRULY ARE--BENEATH THAT SUPPLE FLESH.
YOU ARE HUNGER INCARNATE. UNMOORED BY MORALITY. THE EPITOME OF ***MR. DARWIN'S*** WRITINGS ON PREDATION.

YOU TAKE LIVES AS YOU SEE FIT, LIKE A PREDATOR IN THE DARK.
I DON'T WANT TO ***FUCK*** YOU.
I WANT TO ***BE*** YOU.

SNF.
THERE. AROUND THIS BEND.

I SMELL IT NOW.
MANY VEINS IN UNISON.
IT'S HERE.

THE BLOOD.
AW, HELL. I'M STARTING TO UNDERSTAND THIS MADNESS. IS THAT--?
THE *CHAPEL OF SAN JUAN BATISTA.* IN THE WORLD WE LEFT BEHIND, IT FELL CENTURIES AGO.
IT MATTERS NOT. IT IS A *HOUSE OF GOD.*
AND HIS HOUSE HAS *ALWAYS* OFFERED ME SANCTUARY AND ESCAPE FROM MY PERSECUTORS, EVEN HERE IN *SANGRE DE MORO.*
NO, MR. DIRCK!
I AM LEAVING PERDITION, AND GOING INTO GOD'S LIGHT.
FOLLOW OR DO NOT.

BUT KNOW, THAT UPON OUR RETURN FROM THIS UNHOLY ABYSS, OUR ALLIANCE WILL BE SHATTERED, AND UPON YOU I SHALL DELIVER...

...A FURY MOST RIGHTEOUS...

BIENVENIDOS MIS AMIGOS.
PUEDEN TOMAR ASIENTO.

VENGAN A CELEBRAR NUESTRA ETERNO AMOR.
EL MORO.
NO, ROSA NARANJO, LITTLE COYOTE.

BEHOLD DOMINGO NARANJO'S II' SIZÍINII.
SPIRIT OF A DIVIDED MAN OFFERED TO THE PENUMBRA WITH BLOOD AND BLASPHEMY. UNIFIED BY SKIN AND TOOTH.

I--I HAVE SEEN PUTREFIED LIMBS. LIQUIFIED CORPSES. BUT THAT... THAT...
THE NAG, HER SKIN...
THE BLOOD WAS BAIT!
YOU BROUGHT ME HERE TO SHOW ME THIS?!

YOU WOULD NOT HEAR OUR VOICE.
FOR YOU ARE... OF US, BUT NOT YET... AS US.

I HAD MY SHARE OF RIDDLES AND LIES IN NEW YORK, AND IF YOU THINK YOU UPSET ME, KNOW THAT I VERY REGULARLY HAD TO SEE WILLIAM TWEED NAKED SAVE A MASK.
WHAT DO YOU DESIRE, DEALMAKER?!
HURK

IN THE LAND OF THE SUN MALINGERS A SIGHTLESS SHAMAN.
LURED BY THE LEGEND OF EL MORO, HERZOG JUNG JOURNEYED ACROSS DESERTS BLUE, SEEKING THE CLEVER COURSE RESERVED FOR OUR KIN.

SANGRE. SANGRE. BLOOD OF YOUR FATHER. THE MOOR, NOT MOORISH!
AT SANGRE DE MORO, HERZOG LISTENED FOR EL MORO'S WHISPERS.
"THE BLOOD IS THE LIFE!" OVER AND OVER AGAIN.

JUNG CLAIMED TO SERVE LIKE **THIS ONE** BUT PROVED FALSE, CAGING AND OPENING EL MORO'S VEIN LIKE THE ACEQUIAS IN SPRING.
BUT BLOOD IS THE PATH FROM THE LAND OF THE SUN TO THE DUSK WORLD OF THE ***PENUMBRA.***

ENOUGH BLOOD WILL GUIDE JUNG TO THE ***UMBRA,*** WHERE IT IS ALWAYS NIGHT. WHERE HE CAN TOUCH THE BLACK SKY AND ESCAPE THE FLESH. BECOME ***GREATER THAN US.***
AND ***THAT*** WE CANNOT ALLOW.

YOU WISH ME TO RESCUE EL MORO.
YOU DO ***NOT*** KNOW TO WHOM YOU SPEAK THEN, THING.
AND YOU HAVE TIPPED YOUR OWN HAND.

AS YOU SAY, BLOOD IS THE PATH BETWEEN, SEEPING FROM THE WOUND IN THE WORLD. IT'S HOW I CAME TO BE. IT'S HOW I CAME TO BE HERE.

IT'S HOW WE WILL LEAVE.
HMPH!

WELL? WHAT ARE YOU WAITING FOR? AN ENGRAVED INVITATION?!

I DID NOT KNOW THIS SOUL WHOM YOU KEEP IN TORMENT FOR LONG. BUT I KNEW THE THING HIS BODY BECAME WELL.
HE WAS A WARLORD, AND A CONQUEROR. A MONSTER OF WHICH YOU CAN SCARCELY IMAGINE.
NO.

SLCH
NO. NO. NO. NO.
YOU SHOULD KNOW, CREATURE--MY VOICE WAS BELIEVED TO BE A GIFT AMONG THE HIGHEST CIRCLES OF SOCIETY.
SO, DO CONSIDER IT AN HONOR WHEN I SAY LOUDLY AND EMPHATICALLY...

...FUCK YOU.

UUUOOOT
UUOOOOT!

OH, LORDY AND MY MOMMA, SAVE ME!
UUUOOOT UUOOOOT!

THWAK

TRY AND SCARE ME, WILL YOU?! I'M THE THING IN THE DARK, GODDAMN YOU!
GOT A PRETTY GOOD IDEA OF WHERE THOSE BLOODY THINGS CAME FROM NOW.

SHK
SHK
SHK

WHAT BRINGS YE OUT HERE, SHERIFF WOLFF?
HNH. REVEREND JUNG, MR. O'SHAUGHNESSY. SEEMS HIS RANCH IS FULL OF THESE CRITTERS...DAMNEDEST MONKEYS I EVER DID SEE...

THE REVEREND JUNG TOOK THE WHOLE OF SANGRE DE MORO, FOR WHAT NEFARIOUS PURPOSES I CANNOT SAY. I WAS THE ONLY ONE WHAT DIDN'T GET SWALLOWED UP IN THE CATTLE DRIVE.

CUMBERLAND.

BUT YOU MADE THE PERILOUS TREK ALONE AT NIGHT TO FREE YOUR PEOPLE FROM BONDAGE AND MARCH THEM ACROSS THE DESERT TO THEIR PROMISED LAND.
UH. YEAH. THAT'S ME. LIKE MOSES IN THE GOOD BOOK.

"LOT OF THAT BIBLICAL STUFF GOIN' AROUND."
THE BLOOD IS NOT THE LIFE!

IT IS THE DOORWAY. AND FOR MY CHILDREN WHO PASS THE THRESHOLD, I GIVE UNTO YOU A NEW COVENANT!

WITNESS THE GODSEND!
ONCE HE WAS EL MORO! ONCE HE WAS LEGEND!

NOW HE GIVES HIMSELF TO US!

CHAPTER
V

"IT'S REALLY QUITE SIMPLE.
"THE VAMPIRE WARLORD EL MORO, CAPTURED AND INTERRED IN THAT TOMB BY HERZOG JUNG, IS DRAINED OF HIS TAINTED BLOOD.

"THEN THAT BLOOD IS SIPHONED INTO ONE OF THE CULTIST'S PRISONERS--IN THIS CASE, THE REMAINING RESIDENTS OF SANGRE DE MORO...
"...NOW PSEUDO-VAMPIRES THEMSELVES, THEY ARE IMMEDIATELY EXSANGUINATED...

"...AND THE CONCENTRATED ICHOR--NOW PUMPED INTO THAT POOL--IS, AS WE HAVE SO RECENTLY LEARNED, THE KEY TO PASSAGE BETWEEN WORLDS IN THIS THINLY VEILED PLACE.

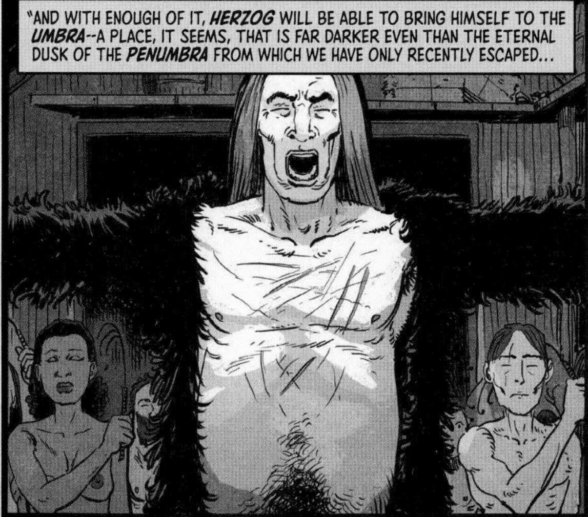
"AND WITH ENOUGH OF IT, HERZOG WILL BE ABLE TO BRING HIMSELF TO THE UMBRA--A PLACE, IT SEEMS, THAT IS FAR DARKER EVEN THAN THE ETERNAL DUSK OF THE PENUMBRA FROM WHICH WE HAVE ONLY RECENTLY ESCAPED...

"...ALLOWING HIM TO BECOME A GOD LIKE THE ONES HE HAS LONG STUDIED...
"...THOUGH IT'S FAIR TO ASSUME HE WILL BE A GOOD DEAL LESS SILENT TO THE PRAYERS OF HIS DEVOTED WORSHIPPERS."

ARE THERE ANY OTHER QUESTIONS, OR HAVE I SUFFICIENTLY TRANSLATED IT FOR THE LESS INTELLECTUAL AMONGST US?

I GET IT. THEY'RE DYIN' AND WE'RE THE ONLY ONES WHO CAN STOP THE CRAZY CUNT WHO'S MURDERIN' 'EM.
BUT HE'S GOT AN ARMY OF PEOPLE MADE UP A' MY FORMER CONSTITUENTS...
AS WELL AS UNTOLD NUMBERS OF THESE BLOOD-DRINKING ***DEMONS.***

DEMONS PERHAPS. BUT ONE DIED BENEATH MY SCALPEL. IF ONE DIES, THEY CAN ***ALL*** DIE--

HEY!
HMPH. I'VE HAD QUITE ENOUGH OF MR. GRIFFIN'S POSTURING.

MISS DER ABEND... WHAT ARE YOU DOIN'?
I'M TAKING WHAT I CAME ALL THE WAY ACROSS THIS COUNTRY FOR.
THE SOIL OF MY BIRTHPLACE, THAT WILL SUSTAIN MY IMMORTAL POWER.

WHATEVER SHOULD HAPPEN TO THESE PEOPLE, WE HAVE NO STAKE HERE ANYMORE, DOOLEY.
THE *STAKE,* MA'AM?! THE STAKES ARE THE *LIVES* OF INNOCENT PEOPLE, ABOUT TO BE BLED OUT BY THEIR FRIENDS 'N' LOVED ONES IN THE NAME OF A MAD PROFESSOR!

THEN, AFTER HE SUCCEEDS, WE WILL HAVE NO TOWN TO GO BACK TO.
GOOD. IT'S JUST THE IMPETUS I NEEDED TO RETURN TO NEW YORK.
I BUILT A LIFE THERE ONCE. I WILL DO IT AGAIN.

WITHOUT YOU, DOOLEY.

UH, WELL, WHATEVER WE'RE MEANIN' TO DO, *MR. O'SHAUGHNESSY,* WE BEST DO IT QUICK! SEEMS THOSE DAMNED MONKEYS DIDN'T TAKE TOO WELL TO WHAT YOU DONE TO THEIR KIN-FELLOWS.

I--I HAVEN'T ALWAYS KNOWN WHAT THE BLOODY HELL I'M DOIN'. BUT I KNOW THE LORD WOULDN'T BRING CHARGES ON THE PEOPLE OF SANGRE DE MORO.
THEN I HAVE JUDGED YOU WRONGLY, BONDSMAN.

I WILL DO AS I HAVE DONE. I WILL SLAY THE *UN-DEAD* AND THEIR KIN. GRIFFIN WILL ASSIST YOU AND THE BRAVE SHERIFF IN YOUR *DIVINE MISSION.*
BUT, *UH--*
GO! I FIGHT ALONE!
SHAK

DO YOU SEE ME, TRUE FATHER?! YOU BORE ME FROM THE DEPTHS OF PERDITION ONCE AGAIN, AND SO I MAKE WAR AGAINST HELL IN YOUR NAME!
BEHOLD!
THE BASTARD OF FRANKENSTEIN COMETH!
POK
POK
POK
POK

♫HEI! HOW SHE SWINGS THE GOLDEN SCOURGE!♪
POK POK POK POK

ROSA.
HNGH!
MY CHILD. I THOUGHT I FELT YOUR PRESENCE, BUT MY MIND IS DELUDED AND WEAK.

JNGL KRAK
JNGL KRAK
I AM MADE GENIZARO ONCE MORE, A SLAVE TO MY OWN THRALL.
YOU MUST FREE ME, ROSA.

WE CAN BE REUNITED AS PADRE E HIJA.
MY LIFE HAS BEEN LONG, AND SO IS MY MEMORY.
YOU WERE NO FATHER. YOU ABANDONED ME BECAUSE YOU THOUGHT I WAS WEAK.
BE PURE, MY BROTHERS AND SISTERS!! YOU FIGHT TEMPTATION! THE POOL BLACKENS LIKE THE SKY!
NO. I SENT YOU AWAY, MI ROSITA...
...BECAUSE I FEARED YOU.

THEY GOT THIS DAMNED THING ALL MOVIN' ON ITS OWN.
AUTOMATION, MY DEAR PADDY. THE WAY OF THE FUTURE. WE NEED TO SHUT IT OFF AT ITS *SOURCE.*
BUT IT'S GUARDED BY THAT *UNSIGHTLY ANNE* WOMAN.

"AND LET ME ASSURE YOU, DESPITE HER EPITHET, SHE SEES *REAL* GOOD."

MAYBE I COULD SHOOT HER DOWN WHILE YOU RUN AT 'EM?
YOU MISSED DIRCK FROM THREE FEET AWAY. ANY MISSTEP WOULD SEND THE CULT UPON US. WE NEED TO GET CLOSER.
WHY ARE THEY WHIPPIN' THEMSELVES?

"THE PAIN KEEPS THEM FROM BEING OVERTAKEN BY THE VAMPIRE'S WILL--AND SERVILE TO JUNG'S MANIPULATIONS. QUITE CLEVER."
GHT!

SO, DISTRACTING 'EM FROM THE PAIN COULD LET EL MORO GET IN THEIR HEADS 'N' FREE HIM SO HE COULD TAKE CARE OF HERZOG HIMSELF. ANY IDEAS?
I HAVE ONE. THERE WAS A PUB IN EAST LONDON WITH A BACKROOM. PEOPLE CAME THERE TO GAWK AND LAUGH AT FREAKS FOR A PENNY A TURN.

NO ACT WAS MORE POPULAR THAN *GHOSTLY GRIFFIN.*

DESTROY THE MACHINE, MR. O'SHAUGHNESSY. I WILL ENTERTAIN THESE TROGLODYTES.

JNGLKRAK
THE GODSEND WEAKENS! HIS TEMPTATIONS FADE AS HIS ICHOR DARKENS!
"I AM THY FATHER'S SPIRIT!"

"DOOM'D FOR A CERTAIN TERM TO WALK THE NIGHT!"
IWA. LES INVISIBLES?

"REVENGE HIS FOUL AND MOST UNNATURAL MURTHER! MURTHER! MURTHER!"
I CAN'T BLOODY BELIEVE THAT'S WORKING.

SHERIFF?

I'LL BE A DOG-- THAT BOOK'S MINE!

GIMME BACK WHAT YOU DONE PLUNDERED, HARLOT!
WHUNGHF!

NO! DO NOT PULL YOUR ATTENTION FROM THE PAIN! YOU WILL ALLOW UNTAMED WORDS INTO YOUR HEART!
HEY, CUNT!

HOW'S *THAT* FER AN UNTAMED WORD?
KRAK
HNK!

O'SHAUGHNESSY?
I'MMA GIVE THAT BOY SOME OF THE FRENCH STUFF FER SURE.

PFAH. YOU WERE THE DREADED EL MORO. YOUR POWER CORRUPTED ALL WHO HEARD YOUR WHISPERS. YOU FEARED NOTHING.
NO, ROSA... ONLY THE LOVE OF YOUR MOTHER KEEPS MY SOUL HANGING BY A THREAD IN THE PENUMBRA.

YOU HAVE NEVER HAD SUCH CONCERNS, ROSA.
YOU ALWAYS TOOK WITH GLEE. NO LOVE EVER HELD YOU IN CHECK.

UNTIL YOU FOUND THIS MAN. THIS DOOLEY O'SHAUGHNESSY. HE GAVE YOU SOMETHING I COULD NOT.

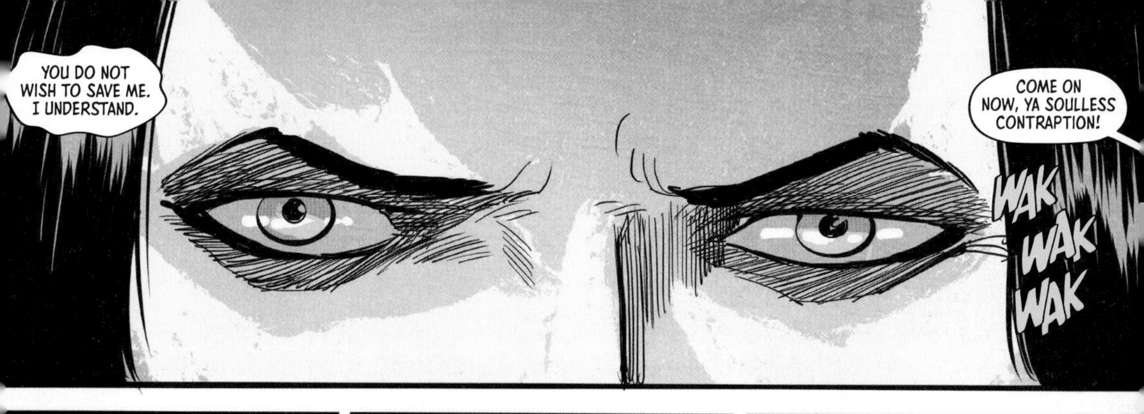
YOU DO NOT WISH TO SAVE ME. I UNDERSTAND.
COME ON NOW, YA SOULLESS CONTRAPTION!
WAK WAK WAK

BUT PERHAPS YOU FIND VALUE IN SAVING THE ONLY BRIDGE TO YOUR HUMANITY YOU HAVE EVER KNOWN.

ENGH HENGH HENNH...

I HEAR HIM IN MY MIND. THE VOICE... SO CLEAR...
MON DIEU... WE...WE'VE BEEN BLIND FOOLS.

TA DA.

NOW, PLEASE LEAVE.
THERE WILL BE NO ENCORE.

YOU. *BOY.*
YOU HEARD THE CALL OF *DER VAMPIR*, LIKE ME.

NOT ONE STEP CLOSER, REVEREND.

DID IT NOT MAKE YOU FEEL WONDERFUL TO BE CHOSEN? TO BE OFFERED SUCH TREASURES. THE BLOOD IS THE LIFE! *THE BLOOD IS THE LIFE!*
I DIDN'T NEED TO EXPERIENCE THE HORRORS TO WRITE 'EM!

I WOULD'VE JUST TAKEN THAT BOOK 'N' RUN! INSTEAD YOU HAD TO STEAL IT, AND DRAG ME INTO THIS GOTDAMN--

--EXHIBITION OF ATROCITIES...

HRRRCH!

BOK
HNF!

MY JOURNAL.
YOU STILL FEEL IT NOW, DON'T YOU...ELATED, PROUD...

UTTERLY BLIND TO REALITY.
HNK!

KRRRR

KRAK
AHHH!
THRADOOOM

LORD ABOVE, IF THE PAIN I ENDURE IS THE PATH YOU HAVE CHOSEN FOR ME, GIVE ME A TRUE SIGN, TRUE FATHER...
...ONE THAT MY CREATOR MIGHT SEE FROM THE PIT IN HELL WHERE HE ETERNALLY DWELLS!
UUUOOOT! UUOOOOT!

KRAKOOOM
GLORY TO THE HEAVENS!

BLACK SHUCK.
THIS IS MY LAND, REVEREND.
NOW YOU'LL PAY FOR YOUR TRESPASS IN BLOOD.
NO! MISS--
DOOLEY, PLEASE, LET ME SAVE YOU.
YOU KNOW HOW I DISLIKE OWING YOU FAVORS.
FWOOMP
HNK!
UNGLAUBLICH. YOU ARE AS I HAVE ALWAYS DESIRED TO BE--THE FIRST TRULY AMERICAN DEITY.
AND AS SUCH...

...YOU WILL
BE CO-OPTED AND
STRIPPED FOR A
PROFIT.

SHLUK

TT.
THE CROSS FROM THE TOP OF THE CHAPEL OF SAN JUAN BAUTISTA. WE FOUND IT WHILE EXCAVATING THE POOL.
THE LAND OF YOUR REBIRTH HOLDS POWER, AS DO THE ITEMS POISONED BY ITS DESECRATION.

YOUR FATHER WAS A GOOD HOST. BUT HE IS SEPARATED FROM HIS SOUL. A HALF BEAST. HIS BLOOD WAS WEAK. IT'S WHY I NEEDED SO MANY OTHER DONORS.
GH.

BUT YOU ARE *PURE* EVIL-- CORRUPTED FROM BIRTH.

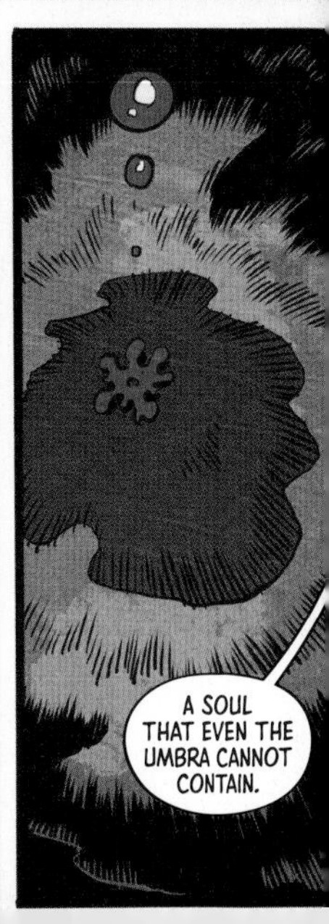
A SOUL THAT EVEN THE UMBRA CANNOT CONTAIN.

MISS DER ABEND!
STOP YOUR SHOUTING. IT'S OVER. SHE'S TOO FAR AWAY, AND THAT RIFLE'S AS BENT AS A LONDON MAYOR.
YEAH. YEAH, IT IS.
Y'KNOW, I WAS AT MANASSAS WHEN THE WAR BROKE OUT. THE COMMANDER, HE WAS YELLIN' "FIRE! FIRE!" I PICKED UP MY RIFLE.
"...I DIDN'T MISS."
I NEVER MISS.

"THE UNION ARMY WAS RUSHIN' AT US, AND I COULD SEE AMONG THEM, THIS BOY. NO MORE THAN ELEVEN OR TWELVE. A LITTLE YOUNGER 'N' YOU."
SO, I AIMED LIKE I'D ALWAYS AIMED WHEN I WAS A BOY, SHOOTIN' RATS OFF THE FENCE FOR MY DINNER. THEY WANTED ME TO FIRE, I WOULD, BUT I WAS GONNA MAKE DAMN SURE I MISSED.
AND THEN...
IN THE HEAT OF THE MOMENT, I'D FORGOTTEN. MY FATHER'S GUN HAD BEEN OLD AND CROOKED. I'D OVERCOMPENSATED.
WITH A STRAIGHT RIFLE I'M A BLOODY AWFUL SHOT.
BUT WITH A CROOKED ONE?
KRAK

OH...
HOW UNFORTUNATE--
NOT FOR EL MORO.
SHNK

KNK
MAGNIFICENT. YOUR THRALL WOULD DO ANYTHING FOR YOU...AND YOU, HIM. AND THAT IS HOW I KNEW YOU COULD FREE ME.
COME, MIJITA. LET US MAKE UP FOR LOST TIME.
HNH!

WE CAN DO MORE THAN SIMPLY SURVIVE. WE CAN MAKE THIS LAND OURS. TAKE BACK OUR NAME.
YOU NEED NOT WALK THE DARKNESS ALONE.
I AGREE, FATHER.
MR. DIRCK?

"DEPART FROM ME, YE CURSED, INTO EVERLASTING FIRE PREPARED FOR THE DEVIL AND HIS ANGELS!"
ROSA?!
NO! I WILL SNAP YOUR BONES! I WILL--
PLSH
ISABEL.
I WILL NOT WALK THE DARKNESS ALONE.
BUT I WILL NOT WALK WITH YOU.
MY JOURNAL, SIR.
=AHEM= YES.

And with that, whatever secret we may have maintained was laid bare for the people of Sangre De Moro.

There were monsters among them.
But they already knew that.

Half their citizens had taken up arms against the other in search of some better world, but had found only betrayal at the hand of their Reverend.
CUMBERLAND... I DON'T KNOW IF...
IF GOD CAN FORGIVE YOU, JOANN, SO CAN WE.

Fortunately HERZOG JUNG was not the only one who had been called by a higher power.

YOU ARE A STRANGER IN YOUR OWN SHELL, PLAGUED BY PAIN AND DOUBT.
IN MY HOUR OF DOUBT, GOD DID NOT ABANDON ME, MY CHILD.

I WILL NOT ABANDON YOU.

Funeral &
APOTHECARY
Neighbors had been lost; their blood spilled into the soil of the mesa.
But new arrivals took their places.

BY THE GREAT HORN SPOON, BOY, IT STINKS TO HIGH HELL IN HERE!
YOU'VE GOT A LETTER, SHERIFF. IT CAME IN WITH MY ORDER.
IT MUST BE FROM AMALGAMATED PRESS, ON THE SUBJECT OF MY PENNY DREADFUL STORY SUBMISSION!

"MR. WOLFF. WE FOUND YOUR SUBMISSION 'OUT BEYOND THE DUST 'N' DARK,' TO HAVE READABLE PENMANSHIP AND YOUR VOCABULARY TO BE FAIRLY ADEQUATE FOR AN AMERICAN.
"UNFORTUNATELY THE WEIRD TALE INVOLVING LEAD CHARACTER OF 'CONNIE DEMORO' WAS AT BEST PREPOSTEROUS, AT WORST BLASPHEMOUS.
"WE SUGGEST YOU RESUBMIT A MANUSCRIPT WITH A SUBJECT THAT MIGHT ACTUALLY RESONATE WITH OUR READERS. CONSIDER, PERHAPS, A HEROIC FRONTIER TOWN SHERIFF..."
BETTER LUCK NEXT TIME, OLD BOY.
I'M SURE FURTHER INSPIRATION WILL COME ALONG.
Miss Der Abend and I had traveled across the young country to escape hunters and reclaim her legacy.

Instead, we found an opportunity to begin a new one.
I'VE TAKEN AN ADDITIONAL PERCENT, A SURCHARGE FOR ASSURING YOU'VE NO BULLETS TO DODGE.
HNPH. I'D BE BETTER OFF WITH THE BULLETS.
MISS DER ABEND.

AFTER YOU INSULTED MR. O'SHAUGHNESSY, I BOUGHT THE TEN CENT GLASS OUT FROM UNDER YOU. I'M TO UNDERSTAND THIS ESTABLISHMENT WAS DIFFICULT TO PROCURE AND ITS LOSS WAS GREATLY UPSETTING.
THE LAND UPON WHICH JUNG BUILT HIS CAMP IS MINE BY BIRTHRIGHT.

DOOLEY SAYS YOU'RE A GOOD MAN, MR. MANOR. TRUSTWORTHY. AND SO, I'D LIKE TO SUPPORT YOUR CLAIM TO THE LAND BELOW THE MESA VIA THE HOMESTEAD ACT. ALL I ASK IS THAT YOU GUARD THAT SOIL...
...AND BE WATCHFUL OF WHAT COMES FROM WITHIN.
YES, MA'AM.

NOW, IF YOU'LL EXCUSE ME, I MUST PREPARE. IF THE TEN CENT GLASS IS TO BE A DESTINATION IN THESE PARTS, IT WILL NEED A MORE REFINED IMAGE.

AND PLEASE... CALL ME ROSA.

IS GRIFFIN YOUR CHRISTIAN NAME OR YOUR SURNAME?
INDEED. A PINT, PADDY. AND AFTER WHAT WE'VE BEEN THROUGH, I'LL ASSUME IT'S ON THE HOUSE.

YOU KNOW, I'VE BEEN THINKING ABOUT WHAT YOU SAID BELOW THE MESA. ABOUT THE 'WEE LAD' YOU SHOT. HOW GUILTY YOU FELT. HOW LOST YOU WERE IN AMERICA, NOT KNOWING WHAT WAS RIGHT OR WRONG.
IT ANSWERED A QUESTION I'VE HAD ABOUT THRALLS LIKE YOU AND REVEREND JUNG.

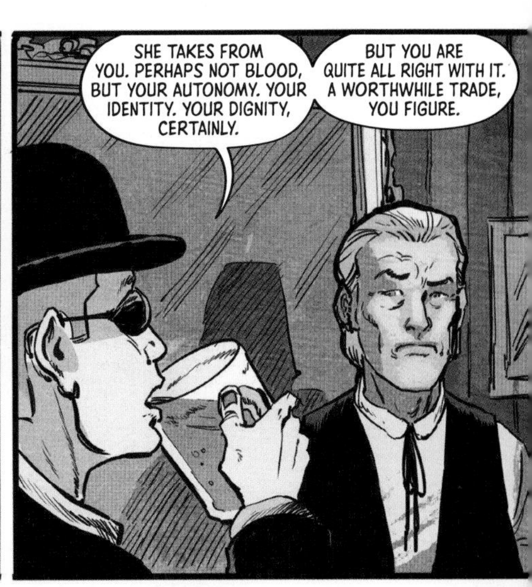
SHE TAKES FROM YOU. PERHAPS NOT BLOOD, BUT YOUR AUTONOMY. YOUR IDENTITY. YOUR DIGNITY, CERTAINLY.
BUT YOU ARE QUITE ALL RIGHT WITH IT. A WORTHWHILE TRADE, YOU FIGURE.

GHK.
BECAUSE SHE HAS POWER. AND HER POWER GIVES *YOU* THE ABILITY TO DECIDE WHO ARE THE ANGELS AND WHO ARE THE DEVILS ***WITHOUT GUILT.***

♫HOJOTOHO! HOJOTOHO! HOJOTOHO! HOJOTOHO!♪
♪HEIAHA HA! HOJOHO!♫
AND THERE IS NOTHING QUITE SO ***AMERICAN*** AS THAT. CHEERS, MATE.

♪TAKE WARNING, FATHER, LOOK TO THYSELF; STORM AND STRIFE MUST THOU WITHSTAND.♫

UTAH TERRITORY.
HNGH. HNGH. HNGH.

HNGH.
SHIT FIRE IN TARNATION, I'M HOME. I'M HOME.

ANNE, MY DEAR. COME IN.
SIR, I'M SORRY, SIR.
I FELL IN WITH THIS FELLA, SEE. AND I...I DIDN'T GET WHAT YOU WANTED.

I'M WELL AND TRULY A WRECK. I'M FALLING APART, SIR.
ON THE CONTRARY, YOUR SURGERY HAS HELD UP FAR BETTER THAN IT SHOULD HAVE.

THIS SANGRE DE MORO IS INDEED POSSESSED OF UNUSUAL PROPERTIES.
BEST, THEN, THAT WE MAKE IT THE POSSESSION OF DR. MOREAU.
FIN?

THE ART OF
SUNDOWN
COVER GALLERY FEATURING
AARON CAMPBELL
TIM SEELEY
JIM TERRY

NO. 1 JIM TERRY
JIM TERRY

WHAT HAS BECOME OF THIS PLACE?

VAULT COMICS PRESENTS "WEST OF SUNDOWN"

They cheered and swooned while SHE spit the blood of one of their own back into their faces!

1

$3.99

vault

WEST OF SUNDOWN

A young country still determining its monsters!

WRITTEN BY SEELEY & CAMPBELL
DRAWN BY TERRY
COLORED BY FARRELL
LETTERED BY CRANK!

CREATED BY SEELEY & CAMPBELL EDITOR-IN-CHIEF ADRIAN WASSEL PUBLISHER DAMIAN WASSEL

SENIOR ARTIST NATHAN GOODEN MANAGING EDITOR REBECCA TAYLOR DIRECTOR OF MARKETING DAVID DISSANAYAKE PRODUCTION BY IAN BALDESSARI ART DIRECTION & DESIGN BY TIM DANIEL

NO. 2 JIM TERRY

NO. 2 AARON CAMPBELL

NO. 3 JIM TERRY

NO. 3 AARON CAMPBELL

VAULT COMICS PRESENTS
"WEST OF SUNDOWN ISSUE THREE"

vault

WEST OF SUNDOWN

She possessed the unholy speed of

SIN!

But it mattred not...

Whether she burned by the sun, or burned by the flame-like the loam that sustained her, she would

BURN!

just the same.

WRITTEN BY
SEELEY & CAMPBELL

DRAWN BY
TERRY

COLORED BY
FARRELL

LETTERED BY
CRANK!

CREATED BY SEELEY & CAMPBELL EDITOR-IN-CHIEF ADRIAN WASSEL PUBLISHER DAMIAN WASSEL

SENIOR ARTIST NATHAN GOODEN MANAGING EDITOR REBECCA TAYLOR DIRECTOR OF MARKETING DAVID DISSANAYAKE PRODUCTION BY IAN BALDESSARI ART DIRECTION & DESIGN BY TIM DANIEL

NO. 4 JIM TERRY

NO. 4 AARON CAMPBELL

VAULT COMICS PRESENTS
"WEST OF SUNDOWN ISSUE FOUR"

vault

WEST OF SUNDOWN

All she needed was to once more bathe in the soil of her

ORIGIN!

WRITTEN BY
SEELEY & CAMPBELL

DRAWN BY
TERRY

COLORED BY
FARRELL

LETTERED BY
CRANK!

CREATED BY SEELEY & CAMPBELL EDITOR-IN-CHIEF ADRIAN WASSEL PUBLISHER DAMIAN WASSEL

SENIOR ARTIST NATHAN GOODEN MANAGING EDITOR REBECCA TAYLOR DIRECTOR OF MARKETING DAVID DISSANAYAKE PRODUCTION BY IAN BALDESSARI ART DIRECTION & DESIGN BY TIM DANIEL

NO. 5 JIM TERRY

NO. 5 AARON CAMPBELL

NO. 1 TIM SEELEY

NO. 1 TIM SEELEY

FIND OUT WHAT LIES BEYOND!
WEST OF SUNDOWN
VOLUME II
IN THE NEW MEXICO TOWN OF SANGRE DE MORO LURKS A VAMPIRE, HER THRALL, FRANKENSTEIN'S MONSTER, AND THE WOULD-BE MAD SCIENTIST.
BUT A NEW THREAT HAS COME FOR THE EVIL-SATURATED SOIL OF THE MESA: ARISTIDE MOREAU AND HIS STRANGE COMPANIONS.
vault